PROHIBITED

**Evernight Publishing**

**www.evernightpublishing.com**

PROHIBITED

# DEDICATIONS

To my beta reader and co-author, Lynn Rae. Writing Prohibited together was an awesome experience! Thank you for suggesting the era. I look forward to many more collaborations, and can't express enough appreciation for your support and guidance in all of my works, no matter my author persona.

—*Peribeth Scott*


For my grandmother, Sarah Margaret Bassett Cron, whose stories about playing the piano between features at the movie theater sparked my interest in the 1920's and 1930's.

—*Lynn Rae*

**PROHIBITED**

# PROHIBITED

## *Forbidden Series, 1*

### Lynn Rae and Peri Elizabeth Scott

### Copyright © 2014

## Chapter One

*Lima, Ohio 1923*

The swell of raucous partying engulfed John MacDonald Adair as he made his way down the stairs from his office and into his covert establishment. He was soon surrounded by men dressed in dark, sober suiting, their faces shiny with sweat and alcohol excess. Women glittered and splashed each section with bright, colorful fabrics, even feathers, and beaded handbags littered the tables alongside tea cups filled with something quite different than that innocuous brew.

Running his long fingers through his thick black hair—he disdained the current fad of using buckets of pomade to slick one's hair back—Mac narrowed his eyes on a certain movement at the bar. Liquor flowed without respite and his staff were kept hopping, but there was a glitch of some sort. He couldn't make it out, and it was time he mingled anyhow. Ensuring his suit jacket fell smoothly around his torso, he shot his cuffs before extending one leg, then the other, to settle the full cuffs of his pants around the polished shoes. He had no need of a mirror to know he looked every inch the confident boss of the establishment. It was a persona he'd carefully cultivated over the years, believing one projected what one *believed*.

"Phillip!"

His head bartender whirled to fix him with a glare, one that immediately softened upon recognizing Mac. His round face shone with sweat, and his tobacco-stained handlebar moustache curled wildly above his chapped lips. "Sir."

"Problem?"

"No, sir. The keg was delivered late and then we were short a man to put it in place."

Mac frowned, then swiftly smoothed out his expression. It wouldn't do to indicate any concern or discomfort. He wouldn't risk either his clientele or staff seeing him as anything less than absolutely and completely in control. It was a heavy burden, but one he didn't care to share with anyone. He alluded to powerful, shadowy partners, which impressed his patrons and enhanced his reputation with cops and politicians on the take. Little did they know he was in it alone.

"How many orders are we waiting for?"

"None, sir. Even the last shipment from Canada arrived. Whiskey. Not watered down either from what I can tell." Phillips reached beneath the counter and concentrated on something just out of Mac's view. When the bartender's hand came into sight it held a small glass half filled with a golden liquid.

"Try this, sir."

Mac didn't drink. As the owner of a speakeasy it was one of those sweet ironies in his life no one else was privy to, and one he'd never divulge. He'd seen enough of his mother's people fall prey to the seduction of alcohol and didn't care to join them in the often horrific consequences. Owning such a place as this didn't serve to convince him otherwise, no matter it made him a very fine living. He took the glass from Phillip and made a of smelling the liquid contained within, waiting for his man to be distracted so he could dump the contents unobtrusively.

"Mac, darling!" His diversion fetched up in a cloud of jasmine scent and a whirl of beads, the golden fabric of her curve hugging dress glowing in the available light.

"Maisie, dear." Mac leaned down to kiss the proffered cheek and found himself locking lips with the buxom blonde. She tasted of gin and tobacco, a blend he managed not to recoil from as her tongue snaked out to forge between his lips. Maisie was welcome in his bed— welcome in many beds if the rumors were true—but he'd avoided kissing her until now.

Smiling in triumph, her eyes sparkling with victory, the flapper dropped one heavily painted eyelid, the lashes clumped with mascara, in a parody of a wink. She tweaked the glass of whiskey from his hand and tossed it back, the long line of her throat working hard above the ropes of beads wrapped around it. The visual made him think of other, carnal things, but he willed his animal response down. She consumed the contents with barely a grimace, and Mac marvelled again at the ability of so many females of his acquaintance to imbibe the way they did.

"See you later, Mac?"

The flavor of her still on his taste buds, he hesitated. Maisie tilted her head and fixed him with a look. He recognized it for what it was and hastily concocted an excuse. "Got shipments coming in later, sweetheart. Work comes first."

Her affronted demeanor melted into immediate comprehension. Maisie understood business. She'd owned her own speakeasy early on before being driven out by male competition and an offer she hadn't been able to refuse. Not that anyone spoke about what transpired—Mac was probably one of the few who knew the truth of that event and he wasn't talking. Nope, as his whisper sister, Maisie could rely on him in that regard, even if he was having second thoughts about her as a lover.

"'Nother time then, Mac," she said with a toss of her head, the tightly curled and pomaded blonde locks impervious to her spirited move.

He watched her sashay between the tables, progress impaired by the casual movements of assorted arms, each covered by dark suit fabric and ending in large, well manicured hands stroking her flanks and thighs. The platinum sparkle of both her hair and jewellery spot-lit her position and drew everyone's eye.

Mac reflected that everything was in order and running as smoothly as possible. All of his shipments, excepting the fictitious ones he'd used to fob Maisie off with, were safely stowed in the warehouse, the police were off his back for now. He'd drop a few hints in well-placed ears over the next few hours to ensure a return of tonight's customers and probably additional ones on the morrow. Nothing like word of mouth to push sales. And if he didn't have anyone in his life to share it with, well, maybe that too would change in the future.

One of those other women in the speakeasy tonight might be a candidate, although inner Mac quailed at the thought of such facile company. Beauty without substance, women frantically living the night life because their daytime lives were no doubt as empty and meaningless. He really needed to get out more, maybe go to a church meeting and meet a type opposite to the flappers. The vagrant thought nearly made him snort. As if one of those women would want to be anywhere near *him*.

Turning to see Phillip observing him with a sardonic gleam in his muddy brown eyes, he nodded to the other man. "I'm gonna step out for a bit. Across the street. Send a boy if you need me for anything. And don't wait a second if you're not sure, Phillip."

"Yes, sir."

Mac eased away from the bar toward the entrance, noting the noise had escalated even within the short period of time he'd been occupied with his bartender and Maisie. He nodded to those who shouted an invitation to join him at their tables, making the ubiquitous "later" signal with his right hand, gaining the door with minimal effort despite the crowd. His muscle, a brute of a man named Dennis, nodded to him, the scar tissue around his eyes making him look even more menacing.

A failed boxer, Dennis gave Mac a form of loyalty that made him feel uncomfortable—hero worship wasn't his deal. He'd merely given the man an opportunity, a job, after finding him in the gutter, soused and broken. Dennis guarded the door with his life, literally.

"I'll be across the street, Dennis. Keep an eye." The other man nodded again, battered face taking on an even more serious mien.

Stepping outside, Mac glanced up and down the nearly empty sidewalks, ill lit in this section of the town by his own design. He felt it both added to the cachet of the speakeasy and made it more difficult to identify those frequenting his establishment. A recent model car racketed by, backfiring as the driver manoeuvred through the gears with a gnashing, grinding sound. Mac's gaze settled on a tall silhouette partially concealed in the jut of the façade on a building directly opposite and with a quick look to his left and right he crossed the poorly surfaced road to approach it.

A thin spiral of smoke wafted around the other man's head, covered with a narrow brimmed hat that veiled the upper half of his face. The vest gaped open at both top and bottom over an ill-fitting shirt that had presumably once been a snowy white, and the suit jacket sleeves stopped just short of knobby, thick wrists. Mac decided not to look at the man's lower body, knowing from experience the trousers would be unpressed and the shoes scuffed and unassuming.

"High time," the cop muttered. "'Bin waiting since one."

"We agreed to meet at two, Finnegan." Mac hid his amusement at the stereotype the name brought to mind. Few Irish made it this far west, preferring the bigger cities of the East. "It's just before the hour."

"Thought you'd be out sooner seeing as there's no more customers making their way in."

Reaching into his inner suit pocket, Mac drew out a sheaf of bills, noting how Finnegan's body went rigid. He supposed the man had been surprised with any manner of threatening items concealed on another's body, but this wasn't one of those times. Dennis was at his back and Mac had another contingency plan in place. As he always did. He offered the wad to the cop who pinched the money between thumb and forefinger in a fastidious gesture at direct odds with his clothing—and his body odor. Shoving the bills into his pocket without counting them Finnegan lifted his chin sharply before shuffling off into the darkness. Just another routine meet on this Friday night. Mac made a mental note to vary the predictability.

Bribing the local cops was part of doing business, and Finnegan wasn't particularly greedy, but he left a nasty impression regardless. Mac raised his hand casually at the two large figures hovering at his peripheral vision and they too drifted into the night. They were another necessary evil, but he wouldn't carry a gat when meeting with a cop. There were some interesting rules about carrying concealed, interpreted loosely by individual policemen, and Mac had no interest in pushing Finnegan's buttons in any way, shape, or form, let alone giving the man any additional power over him. Having two street fighting men at his back gave him necessary security.

As he crossed the threshold of the speak, Mac was assailed by a memory of his past as the close atmosphere inundated his senses.

*Little John Adair wrinkled his nose at the stench emanating from the outhouse. The tiny building adjacent to his humble abode was all he'd ever known for relief in his short life until the brief visit to his auntie's home in Lima, where something known as a water closet enhanced life considerably. There were other things in Aunt Louisa's home too. Electric lights instead of oil lanterns replaced the old gas fittings, not that the shack he called home had even those.*

*Little John listened intently as his mother spoke with her half sister about all the modern conveniences she'd acquired since marrying her white husband. They'd seen him at that point, and shooed him out to play with the little brown dog sporting an engraved leather collar. Even the animals were rich here. Little John had his first taste of wealth and influence and embraced it. That was probably the beginning of his rejection of his culture, although he never forgot his roots.*

Breathing deeply to fill his lungs with the stew of rich scents pervading the speakeasy and pushing the other olfactory memory aside, he reached the heavily embellished wooden bar, the polished surface now marred with a variety of spilled liquids. He stared around him with pride, if not contentment.

Windows had been cut into the thick walls of the speak and functioned well to deal with the stench of revelry and the faint effluvium of used motor oil sometimes drifted up from the concrete floor despite the covering of heavy planks of resilient redwood hauled in from the Pacific coast on one of Lima, Ohio's many railway lines. The high ceilings were festooned in drapes of black fabric designed to capture the cacophony of noise erupting from dozens of female and male throats drowning out the frantic efforts of the piano player.

Hoping the "orchestra", a motley crew of black musicians he secretly wondered if he could foist on his current patrons would soon arrive to support the floundering key pounder, Mac hung onto his satisfaction. Club profits were at an all time high. The automotive plants that had churned out trucks for use in the European War gave Lima's inhabitants the very possibly false impression of continuing riches. Mac's business was quite different than manufacturing motor trucks or refining oil, but no less lucrative.

Most people riding high on the good times didn't think further than stuffing their wealth under the mattress and Mac sometimes found himself thinking the same when caught up in the rush of easy money.

Didn't matter though. He was a capitalist at heart and would take advantage of the current beliefs. It was insane that a person might drink in the privacy of his own home without any recourse but people couldn't get together and do so—enter Mac's speakeasy. He'd bought the old warehouse for a song and refurbished it cheaply even as he paid fair wages to local laborers, Shawnee, white and black alike. He was an equal opportunity employer, hiding his largesse behind the assumption he'd take advantage of the poor and uneducated like every other businessman.

Phillip was observing him again, visibly wondering if Mac had dealt with whatever issue drawing him outside, probably worried because he appeared so deep in thought. Those who worked for him were fiercely loyal and discreet, and he rewarded those qualities. While he was nothing like his warrior family roots, he didn't hesitate to call on his warrior instincts when the need arose. Mac kept that side of his life a secret. The KKK was also alive and well in Lima, and while they might just barely tolerate music from black folk, he doubted they'd support a half breed Shawnee running a successful speakeasy, rubbing shoulders with the local politicians, rich white folk, and fun seekers each and every evening, treating him as their equal.

He nodded at the man in reassurance, then strolled between the crowded tables, nodding and smiling at his patrons, squeezing the male shoulders of those more familiar to him.

"Mac!" One of the local politicians motioned him over, bonhomie written all over his florid face. A well-endowed brunette rested her breasts on the man's forearm, blinking blearily up at Mac, her face heavily made up to match the shimmering, beaded fabric of her gown.

"Hello, Maury. Elise."

"Sit and stay awhile, my friend!" Maury motioned for the whole table to be served and Mac nodded to

15

Phillip. He'd be served his tall glass of water with a slice of lemon to represent gin—the bartender accepted he never drank with patrons, only sampled the goods to establish their veracity. Mac smiled ruefully to himself. He had many plates spinning all at the same time.

The evening wore on until the patrons finally tired and made their way to their various homes, leaving Mac to count the receipts before he could find his own— empty—bed. It would be dawn before he made it to his new mansion across town in a neighborhood quite different than the present locale.

## Chapter Two

"Get a wiggle on Lilly, the fellas'll be here in a flash."

Lillian Townsend wanted to glare at her cousin but since she'd just been powdered, kohled, and rouged within an inch of her life, she wasn't going to risk making a wrinkle in the fine mask now covering her face. Instead, she glanced at the younger woman from the reflection of the vanity mirror as Annie Beechly pulled and rolled her stockings, twisting this way and that as she checked the fancy clocks and garters nearly visible under the hem of the sparkling tangerine evening dress.

"I'm not sure why we're putting so much effort into our appearance. Didn't you say this establishment was in an old mechanic's shop?"

"I did but it's the hottest place in town now, cuz. Stand up and let me see you."

At her cousin's urging, Lilly rose from her seat on the carved bench and turned around. She'd refused most of Annie's fashion advice that started with lopping off her wavy chestnut hair and ended with taking a pair of scissors to her favorite emerald green silk evening gown. Instead of such drastic measures, Lilly merely pinned her hair up in a roll imitating the curl of a bob and fixed it with a pearled comb and allowed her cousin to apply makeup with a free hand. She was wearing her most daring gown. Granted, the dress wasn't especially fashionable, but it was made from lovely blue Chinese brocade and it did scoop low in the back, lower than any other selection in her wardrobe. Certainly elegant enough for the patrons of a rough speak on the wrong side of the tracks in Lima, Ohio.

Annie rustled over and busied herself with tweaking sapphire blue folds and pleats as Lilly glanced around the large bedroom her aunt and uncle had provided her and wondered what sort of emergency items she should stuff into her mesh evening bag. Money, handkerchief, sal volatile in case someone fainted, nail file, anything else? With a sigh, she glanced at her favorite overstuffed reading chair perfectly placed by the bow window and the stack of books waiting for her on the inlaid table next to it. She knew by the end of the evening she would decide she'd have been better off staying home and reading the farm foreman's letter and going over the accounts, but she'd promised Annie she'd go. When Walter Bushnell had found out where they were heading, he'd insisted on coming along to protect them from the mixed and unpredictable crowd. Oh, Walter. What was she going to do about him? And why was she wasting a perfectly good Saturday night at a speakeasy?

"You look divine even if that dress is about five inches too long. You have great gams, Lil, why not show them off?"

"Because I use my legs for locomotion not provocation." Lilly knew she sounded like a prude, but she was hardly going to alter a perfectly serviceable garment to follow a passing fad. What would she wear when hemlines went back down as they surely would next year? She couldn't say anything of the sort to Annie though, because she'd get an earful from the younger woman about why one would worry about such things when the money was pouring in and shopping was so much fun?

"They can do both things at once. Mine certainly do." Annie smiled and pirouetted, her flanged skirt flaring out and sparkling as she turned. She really was adorable with her shiny blonde hair and bright blue eyes made even more alluring with a smudge of smoky black along her lashes. Annie would turn every head in the place, giving Lilly the opportunity to stay quiet and survive the evening with as few awkward encounters as possible. Other than fending off Walter and his increasingly heavy attempts to cement their association. Everyone from her aunt and uncle, her charitable associates, and the young man himself were convinced he was the perfect prospect to entice the young widow Mrs. Daniel Townsend from behind her veil of mourning and return her to the bustle of society.

Interrupting her thoughts, a car horn bleated loudly from outside and Annie rushed to the open window, shouting through the screen they were on their way. With a squeal of excitement, she skipped from the room and clattered down the wide stairs leaving Lilly to collect their handbags, gloves, wraps, and inform the irritable housekeeper they'd be out for the evening. Mrs. Kessler lowered her gray eyebrows and harrumphed as if Lilly had told her she and Annie were going to strip to their step-ins and march along Market Street while tooting kazoos.

"I hope you two don't galumph in here at an odd hour of the morning, I can't be held responsible for what sort of breakfast you'll get if I don't have enough sleep." The older woman shook her head as she followed Lilly down the wide hallway toward the open door Annie had left in her wake. Lilly tried not to shudder as she contemplated how the surly woman might make eggs and toast inedible. She couldn't stop her stomach from contracting at the thought.

"I'm sure we'll be home at an entirely reasonable hour, Mrs. Kessler. And I'll do my very best to keep everything quiet."

"See that you do. I'd hate for Mr. and Mrs. Beechly to be disturbed, seeing's how they're off at the fundraiser this evening, doing the Lord's work." Mrs. Kessler's worshipful admiration of Annie's parents had always struck Lilly the wrong way even before she'd come to live under their roof and had daily encounters with the housekeeper. Not for the first time she wished she'd stayed at the farm and avoided coming to town entirely.

Lilly grasped the front door's heavy brass handle as she contemplated how attending a casino night at the country club could in any way be viewed as Christian charity. Unless one placed the rarified club members in the needy category, which she most certainly did not. She had a suspicion that if the attendees of the party simply pooled the money they'd spent on new clothes, jewels, and gambling tokens, they would have enough money to fund an entirely worthy endeavor for a month or more. No, the idea of spending the evening among the well-connected and well-satisfied denizens of Allen County held little appeal for her, which was why she'd chosen the lesser evil of going to a shady speakeasy with her spitfire cousin instead. Lilly doubted she'd encounter anyone there who knew what a cotillion even was, or a tea dance, or a musicale.

Shutting the heavy, carved oak door firmly behind her, Lilly stepped along the paved walk toward the curb where a large green touring car waited, its white wall tires and canvas top gleaming like beacons in the light of streetlamps. Annie was already in the backseat with Raymond Diller, her special friend of the moment, which left Lilly to take her place in the front next to Walter. Even though Walter was distantly related to her late husband Daniel, he was a pale substitute. His hair was lighter, his sense of humor less fun, his personality less forceful than the man she'd lost four years ago. He certainly didn't light much of a fire within her and she wasn't willing to compromise on that. She'd had love once and wouldn't settle for convention's sake.

"Lil, you look divine," Walter complimented as he handed her in to the car, a lone streetlamp's beam making his slicked-back hair shine as though he'd been dipped in fresh crude oil. Lilly nodded at his comment as she handed Annie's accessories back to her, her cousin's mesh bag stuffed with makeup and probably cigarettes, and then neatly stowed her own on her lap. Walter pulled out onto the wide boulevard with another bleat of the horn and sped along Market and across the trolley tracks, to turn south towards the more industrial side of town, the road surface changing from smooth and clean to more rutted and littered with every block he drove. She clutched the sides of her stool-like seat, envying Annie and Ray's more secure bench in the back. Walter always drove like he was trying to impress everyone with his speed and skill, likely to add luster to his aspirations to open his own automobile dealership. He only managed to make her slightly sick to her stomach on every trip.

Soon the buildings around them shifted from increasingly smaller and drabber residences to tall brick structures with narrow glass windows. There was an aroma of hot metal and burned coal in the air as he circled a particular block looking for a place to park among the wide assortment of vehicles crowding the curbs. It seemed a lot of people were still at work. Lilly sighed as she looked at the manufacturing plants surrounding them, all filled with people working late into the night to feed their families, while spoiled and useless folks like herself were off to have mindless fun.

As they exited the vehicle, Lilly noticed most of the buildings were well-lit and noisy with the clang of machinery as the workers spewed out automotive parts or cigars or rolls of twine. Walter and Raymond eagerly discussed the latest baseball scores as Annie captured Lilly's arm and rolled her eyes. Either her cousin was sweet enough on Raymond to be amused by his enthusiasms, or she was growing bored with the earnest young man. Lilly had a sneaking suspicion it was the latter and she anticipated a messy breakup in the future.

Kicking aside crumpled paper and cigarette butts, they walked along a narrow alley between two tall buildings, crossed another street and reached a peeling gray door set in a nondescript whitewashed brick wall. Walter favored her with an arched eyebrow as he raised his fist to knock three times with long pauses between strikes, his mild gray eyes alight with the drama of the moment.

There was no response.

"Sure we're at the right door?" Raymond glanced around the dark and deserted street. Lilly did as well, wondering where the stream of well-dressed folk hoping to obtain alcohol and a good time might be. Her skin contracted into goose pimples as her nerves increased.

"This is right, old Cal showed it to me yesterday when we down here doing a test drive." Walter frowned at the door and hit it three more times.

"Still working on that dealership idea?" Annie piped up, a smile on her pinked lips. Lilly shot her a warning look, not interested in hearing her cousin yet again badger Walter about his prospects. Annie, alone among Lilly's friends, was convinced Walter was simply after Lilly's money and her body, in that order. Lilly thought both were uninteresting topics.

"You bet. I've almost decided the manufacturer. It's either Winton or Cleveland—"

A sharp creaking sound interrupted him and they all turned to look at a small panel that had opened in the door. A dark eye peered out at them and Lilly held her breath, tense with uncertainty. Would they be admitted or not?

The little portal shut with another squeal and a definite click, immediately followed by the slow opening of the thick door. A burly man in a dark suit nodded at them and swung his hand out to welcome them inside. Lilly noted how battered his face appeared and wondered how that had come about. As the rest of her party rushed inside with laughter, she hesitated, certain she was going to regret this experience for some reason. Her belly tightened and her skin prickled almost as if she was suddenly in the grip of an ague. It must be guilt. What was a card-carrying member of the Women's Christian Temperance Union doing entering a clandestine club in the business of selling outlawed substances?

Giving herself a shake and reminding herself her aunt and uncle were depending on her to keep an eye on their increasingly wild daughter, Lilly entered the dim foyer. She jumped as the door shut behind her and realized she'd passed the point of no return.

Following Annie's glittering hem down a dark hallway that smelled of tobacco smoke, Lilly stopped dead when she entered a large room packed with laughing people of all manner of dress and appearance, lifting drinks with gusto. Black cloth cloaked the ceiling in a funereal tent and a small musical group sawed out an up tempo ragtime ditty to the apparent delight of some gyrating couples crowded on a dance floor. Well-dressed and raucous men and women circled round tables covered with innumerable white china cups rather than the assorted glassware she'd expected. Perhaps the pottery was sturdier than the delicate crystal drinkware crowding the cabinets at her aunt and uncle's. The sharp tang of raw alcohol filled the air along with thick coils of cigar smoke and she couldn't help wrinkling her nose. Perhaps the country club might have been a better choice.

Walter grabbed her elbow and pulled her along towards an unoccupied table at the other end of the space. Lilly tried not to trip over sprawling legs or bump into people as they laughed and staggered across her path, but she nearly overbalanced on her jeweled heels several times before she reached the slight safety of the table where Annie and Raymond waited.

"Drinks, my man," Walter announced with a possessive clap on the tabletop. Raymond followed him to the bar lining the nearby wall. Glancing at them as they left, Lilly's attention was diverted when she noticed a tall, swarthy man leaning against the surprisingly ornate wooden bar. As if he could sense her gaze, he swiveled his head her way and focused his startling eyes on hers. A bright, clear blue, they seemed so out of place in his tanned face. Her whole body jolted like she'd fallen against the wire of the electric trolley car that ran past her aunt and uncle's house. For one breathless moment, everything went quiet in Lilly's world as they locked eyes.

"Lil, take a peek at that!" Annie's excited cry jolted her out of her odd reverie and Lilly forced herself to concentrate on what bit of fluff had caught her cousin's fancy. With a breath of relief she looked away from the staring stranger with the broad shoulders. As she followed where her cousin's red-tipped fingers extended, all she could see were flush-faced people shimmying on the dance floor in front of the admittedly very talented band.

"They're playing that new song, the one about bananas. Oh, I've got to get out there and dance to it before it's over. Raymond! Come on!" Annie called out to her friend in a high-pitched squeal and Lilly fought the urge to cover her ears.

Ray appeared at the table and dropped the mugs he'd been carrying to the tabletop as the liquid inside sloshed over the thick rims. Her cousin scooped hers up and drained it in one smooth move as her companion did the same. They clicked empty mugs together just before Ray swept Annie up in his arms and nearly carried her to the dance floor. At a more stately pace, Walter arrived and deposited two more drinks on the damp table. Lilly frowned.

"Walter, you know I don't—"

"I know, baby, but it's expected here. We have to keep up appearances."

Lilly tightened her lips rather than respond as she would have liked. It was hard to fathom how it would be possible to have elevated standards of behavior in such a place. She counted herself lucky to have found a seat with four legs.

Walter took a quick drink, his Adam's apple bobbing as he swallowed. He glanced around the room and Lilly knew he was seeking out men of influence he could attempt to impress. He was no different here than whenever he escorted her to a country club function. Come to think of it, she had recognized a few faces from the church pew and lecture hall here, so it was no wonder Walter was on the make. Lilly wondered who recognized her, and how they'd react to each other at the next ice cream social or tea dance.

"Oh, say, there's City Commissioner Cunningham. I need to pigeonhole him about the lot on the corner of Elizabeth and High. Care to come along?"

Shaking her head, Lilly declined. "It's better if I stay here. We might lose our table if it's empty." That part was true. It was so crowded in the noisy space she

25

was surprised no one had taken a seat on the edge of their table. In fact, so many people had surged forward to watch the band perform she couldn't even see the bar anymore or the dark man who'd stood there moments before. He seemed the sort to keep a wary eye on, and she glanced around but didn't spy him anywhere.

Walter shrugged and left with a spring in his step and his mug in hand. Nothing cheered him more than rubbing elbows with influential people.

Lilly concentrated on the band. She was surprised to see the members, other than the thin piano player, were black, but their frenetic arrangement of the newly popular song claimed all her attention. They'd somehow worked a syncopated backbeat in with the jaunty melody and she strained to catch the notes. It seemed most of the people dancing didn't care about the race of their entertainers, judging by their enthusiastic movements and shouted accompaniments to the lyrics. It was a sad fact that most of the people enjoying the band's talents wouldn't dream of acknowledging one of its members if they came upon him walking in Farout Park the next day. She caught a glimpse of Annie's pale orange dress in the blur of dancers as the band moved into another equally up-tempo song without taking a break.

Twisting her lips as she suppressed a smile triggered by her cousin's enthusiasm, Lilly pushed the mug of liquor meant for her to the middle of the table as she tried to ignore the prickling feeling growing on the back of her neck.

\*\*\*\*

"Not to your taste?" A deep voice caressed her ear and Lilly tilted her head up to see the man from the bar standing too close to her. Far too close. He was wearing a light gray suit that draped over his body with pressed seams and perfectly placed hems. The overall impression he made was that of lean strength. One of his eyebrows arched up at her as he scanned her face.

"What?" Lilly's skin prickled and she could only take in a shallow breath. He stared down at her like a wolf would contemplate a quivering rabbit. She couldn't decide if she should run or stay still and hope he would move on to other prey.

"Your drink. It's not to your liking?"

"No." She could barely get the tiny word out from between her paralyzed lips.

"I don't believe you." His disdain snapped her out of her strange immobility. She'd seen that expression on many men's faces, when she'd marched for suffrage, when she'd spoken against liquor, when she'd campaigned for innumerable charities. That dismissive look said she was a silly woman who didn't know her mind and her lot would be better if she'd just stay quiet and let men run things as nature intended. Take her appropriate place in the kitchen and the bedroom. Anger burned away her frozen nerves.

"Your opinions are of no interest to me, *sir*, no matter how erroneous they are."

His lips curled back and he bared his teeth at her like the wolf he resembled. "Fancy words I happen to understand just fine. Do you think you're going to scare me off by going all high-hat?"

"What you do and where you go are none of my business." As much as it pained her, Lilly looked away from his crystalline eyes and fastened her attention on the dancers, the band, the portly man coughing at the next table, anything to make the brush-off as clear as she could while seated alone at a small table in an uproarious speakeasy. If he had an ounce of manners he'd take himself away and leave her in peace. Her heart thudded in her chest and she slipped her hands onto her lap and

27

under the table so she could twist her shaking fingers together.

"Oh, but what you do here *is* my business."

Lilly blinked in shock as he lowered his impressively tall body onto one of the unoccupied chairs and adjusted his cuffs and sparkling links. With a practiced move of his large hand he smoothed his red and black silk tie. After clearing his throat, he picked up the mug she'd rejected and gave it an elaborate sniff. How uncouth! But what else could she expect from someone so clearly at ease in this hedonistic environment? He didn't even seem to notice the people surrounding him or the music beating through the air like a flock of singing birds.

"What are you doing? I didn't invite you to join me and I certainly don't wish you to inspect my drink." Lilly hoped outrage was clear in her tone, but her voice betrayed her with a breathy squeak.

"Seems fine. You need something more expensive to wet your whistle? French champagne perhaps?"

"Absolutely not!"

With deliberate slowness, he returned the mug to the table, leaned her way and stared. Lilly's throat tightened on anything else she might have said as the stranger's gaze heated her skin. She wished for her gloves, her wrap, anything to cover her arms and modest décolletage. He spread his legs and propped his elbows on his knees as he looked her over like she was a steak he just might select for dinner.

"Aren't you going to dance?"

"No." Lilly wanted to squirm back in her seat. He was too close; knees almost touching hers, hands dangling a few inches on either side of her thighs, face close enough she could see his thick, dark eyelashes. Her internal temperature shifted from cold to hot in an instant and she shuddered. Perhaps she *was* growing ill. "You don't approve of the band?" His mouth curved as he cocked his head back.

Lilly shook her head in an attempt to clear it, unable to tear her gaze from his.

"Too dark for your taste?" The stranger was scowling now, all bunched eyebrows and glare communicating his disapproval.

With a start, Lilly realized he thought she was prejudiced. With a sniff and a straightening of her spine, she defended herself from his terrible implication. "Yet again, you are completely in the wrong."

His somber face shifted and he leaned against the chair's back as it creaked in protest. His jacket fell away from his broad chest and the pristine white fabric of his shirt glowed in the low light of the club. "Really?"

She frowned at him and gave him a curt nod. *What cheek!* "Of course. Why are you convinced I'm a liar?"

"I don't know, maybe the fact you're seated so comfortably at an illegal club? Someone who flouts the law can't be very trustworthy."

All of Lilly's pent-up guilt over being there flushed heat through her body and she knew her cheeks were now glowing red with shame. Her knees trembled and she felt more ill at ease than she had speaking to the Lotus Club last week. Her chosen platform had been the social and economic necessity of access to reproductive controls and no matter how carefully she'd couched her terms describing condoms, pessaries, and menstrual cycles, many of the ladies in the audience had turned as beet red as she knew she was now. Although why she'd thought of contraceptives while being badgered by this stranger was inexplicable.

While she struggled for something to say, he glanced away from her and looked up. Lilly started when a hand gripped her shoulder, but she recognized Walter's cool fingertips and the sharp scent of his bay rum cologne with a sigh of relief. Or was it annoyance?

"Lil, sorry I was delayed. Who's this?" Walter said with a slur. He'd had a few more mugs of liquor with the city commissioner, it seemed. She should be grateful he'd returned to distract the other man, but a small tremor of disappointment fluttered in her chest. Now she wouldn't be able to say something wildly cutting to the arrogant man who remained seated as he evaluated Walter. After a few leisurely moments, he rose and shook Walter's outstretched hand.

"I'm Mac Adair. This is my place." Lilly's whole being flushed with embarrassment before she regrouped, all the while avoiding the *owner's* eyes. No matter his status, he'd had no call to speak to her that way.

Walter introduced himself and forgot to include Lilly. That suited her just fine. The less interaction she had with judgmental Mr. Mac Adair, the better.

"That's jake! Good to meet you. Thanks for keeping my baby company while I was gone." Walter eased his hand away from Lilly's shoulder as he maneuvered into the seat the other man had just vacated. Mr. Adair's knowing gaze watched Walter's fingers slide from her skin and he again quirked that swooping eyebrow at her. Lilly swallowed back her impulse to tell Walter to stop calling her baby since it was demeaning. She'd mentioned it often and he conveniently didn't listen each time. "Lots of the rougher sort bumping around in this place and I'd hate for her to be mashed on by some lout."

"No shortage of impolite folk anywhere you go these days," Mac Adair commented while he stood, feet braced apart as laughing and swizzled men and women surged past him to get to the dance floor.

The band had upped the volume while he'd been haranguing her and it seemed like everyone was in a mad dash to participate. None of the revelers bumped in to him, no drinks spilled on his fine grey suit, and he acted as if he didn't even notice them as he watched Lilly watching him. His expression was difficult to interpret. Was it dislike? Superiority? Her insides curled like she had eaten a bad oyster and cold flushed along her skin again. He dipped his chin at her and turned away without saying another word. Impolite folk indeed.

\*\*\*\*

Concentrating on maintaining a casual, aloof demeanor, Mac eased through the scattered tables, avoiding the shuffling mass of people approaching or leaving the small dance floor. It cost him, but he didn't look back at that ritzy sheba who'd held court all by her lonesome until that sap hustled back the instant Mac sat down.

He'd seen the man coming—had he introduced himself? Mac didn't remember. He'd been busy beating his gums and acting like an ass when he realized the guy was with her and returning to establish his claim. What possessed him to hassle—Lil? Was that her name? A nickname? He knew he'd overstepped and made some assumptions about her being a snob and prejudiced. She'd been so … appalled by his abruptness.

Maybe it was because she was sitting by herself, regal and cool, wearing what could only be termed a wildly conservative gown amongst the immodest apparel showcasing all the other women in his establishment. She didn't fit. Instead, with her elegantly coifed chestnut hair—no tortured curls and frizz for *Lil*—she shone, head and shoulders above the crowd and he'd been overcome with a bizarre need to protect her. Drive her out of a place so obviously unsuitable for a Jane like her.

He might have achieved his goal, forced her out. After all, he'd been a cad—because this wasn't the place or time. Hell, there'd never be a place or time. She was far beyond Mac Adair's aspirations. He might be wealthy and he knew he looked the part, but that kind of woman wouldn't normally give him a second glance. She was the stuff of country club events, destined to be on the arm of some classy guy with a job that didn't raise any eyebrows. Yet the way she cheeked him right back! He hadn't intimidated her at all. A feisty woman who stirred him, when he preferred the cute, chippy type. Like Maisie.

"Sir?" Phillip posed a question with his eyes.

Mac started. He'd found his way back to the bar—literally had his back against it—without even realizing.

"We're closing early tonight. Tell the wait staff to convey the message and you tell the patrons when they come to the bar."

"Closing early?" The bartender's face might have been comedic any other time, but Mac was feeling edgy, something uncommon for him unless something alerted his senses and wanted the place cleared sooner than later.

To convey a sense of certainty, a far cry from how he was actually feeling—he'd never felt quite so stymied in his life—he cudgelled his brain for a response.

"The police are rumored to be making their rounds in this area. If we're cleared out by two, three at the latest, they won't hear anything and have no reason to check."

Phillip nodded instantly, conveying his understanding and appreciation for Mac's caution. "We'll sell bucketfuls once the customers hear of the early closing," he opined. "Wouldn't want to go home without a snoot full."

Well, there was that. It wasn't Mac's intent, but money was money. He chanced a casual look back at Lil's table. Cool as an ice princess, the blue brocaded stuff of her dress shimmering with class, a butterfly amongst the brash moths. And he was getting fanciful. Dizzy for a dame. Pah. That wealth of hair, so perfectly rolled and fixed, cried out for someone's hands to loosen and sift their fingers through it. Not his, of course.

Tossing her head in the style of a spirited thoroughbred, Lil scooted her chair away from that possessive type. Maybe they were getting ready to leave. Mac narrowed his eyes and sought to analyze their relationship. Were they a couple? And why did he care?

"Gonna pace the room, Phillip. Get the word out."

Working the crowd again, he tenaciously kept his back to Lil and the sap. Maisie hovered before him wherever he went and he knew she was questioning yet another excuse not to meet up. Two nights in a row was obviously testing her patience. Well, the early closing should put paid to that. Maisie would find another speak and dance until dawn. He was no longer interested in a good time girl who shared her favors.

But he wouldn't risk a scene by refusing Maisie without cause. They shared some unspoken secrets. He took on the task of dropping the word into the ear of at least one patron at each table he schmoozed with. Their disappointment that the evening would be coming to a close was voluble. And, as Phillip predicted, there was a rush on the bar and imperious waves to the servers.

As he rounded the last table he cast his eyes toward where Lil sat, telling himself she'd surely be gone and forgotten. But there was another couple seated with her and her date, the woman a tarted-up blonde very

33

familiar with the man she snuggled against. Mac checked the status of Lil's physical connection to—what the hell was his name? His gut relaxed and he let out a breath he hadn't realized he'd been holding when he noted how Lil held herself separate. No mauling for her. Did she feel different from the other people here? As different as she looked? The way he felt different despite his efforts to fit in?

Mooning over a bird, no matter how much of a peach she was, simply wasn't his style and he tore his gaze away, chastising his brain and certain parts of his anatomy to calm down and focus. He assumed Lil was quick and bright. He *knew* she was beautiful and classy and he was a half-breed who ran a speakeasy. When he next looked—purely because that table was in his direct line of vision—she was gone. The pang of loss shook him. He pushed it down and locked it away with all the other disappointments in his life and concentrated on his business. He'd be nothing without it and there was nothing else in his life but business. It wasn't like he'd ever see her again.

## Chapter Three

Lilly looked over the creamed beef on toast congealing on her plate and an accompanying glass bowl of pineapple in heavy syrup with some outrage. She and Annie had come home the evening before at a decent hour and she was certain they hadn't made excessive noise. Lilly had removed Annie's velvet heels at the front door and slid off her own satin ones at the same time. Yet Mrs. Kessler still exacted her punishment by creating this horror. After the evening she'd had, breakfast felt like the last straw and she couldn't decide if she should head to the kitchen and lose her temper or rush back to her room for a good cry. She sniffed and poked her fork in the grayish sauce covering shreds of stringy beef as she considered her options.

It was the fault of that man, Mac Adair. He'd insulted her, agitated her, and she was still feeling the aftereffects, even after a restless night's sleep. Unwelcome images of his knowing expression intruded on her thoughts constantly, when she'd tried to fall asleep, when she'd awoken, as she'd bathed her face and pulled on her day dress. She could almost see him leaning back in one of her aunt's new Chippendale dining chairs as he smirked at her before sipping some coffee from a fine porcelain cup. She must have shaken her head because her aunt stopped spreading jam on a biscuit and widened her eyes.

"Lilly, whatever is the matter?"

"Nothing, Aunt Eula. Just regretting a few things this morning."

"Ah, your escapade with Annie wasn't as much fun as you'd hoped?"

Lilly's mouth fell open and all thoughts of Mac Adair fled her mind for the first time since she'd met him.

Annie had been sure her parents would never know where they'd gone the night before. She'd carefully explained they were staying in to listen to some new records on the Victrola when Eula and Wendell had left the night before. It seemed her little cousin wasn't that good of a schemer, which was a relief in a way.

"Escapade?" Lilly was careful not to confirm anything. She reached for her coffee cup and it rattled in the saucer as she lifted it. Nerves about being found out, *not* random thoughts about some rude man's fingers as he flexed them against his knees so close to hers.

"Of course. You two went with Walter and Ray to that speakeasy on the south side. If that's not an escapade I don't know what is. Mrs. Crumrine called first thing this morning simply thrilled to gossip." Aunt Eula shook her head and went back to embellishing her lopsided biscuit. Mrs. Kessler had supplied her usual tasteless lumps that morning but Eula never seemed to notice her housekeeper had a terrible hand with baking. And cooking in general for that matter.

"She did?"

Eula nodded, her carefully pinned, graying hair gleaming in the light of the stained glass fixture over the breakfast table. "I hardly expect you to restrain Annie when she's determined to have her way. I'm pleased you went with her and took the boys. For protection. It couldn't have been easy for you to step foot in the place."

Her uncle rattled his newspaper and lowered a corner to glance Lilly's way, his one visible brown eye bright with amusement. "All sorts down there. Negroes, bootleggers, boiler stokers, crab apple chuckers, who knows what. You girls could have ended up riding in a freight car with some hobos all the way to San Francisco."

Lilly smiled at him. Uncle Wendell was such a card. "I doubt we could have climbed up into one between our fancy shoes and narrow skirts."

"Saved by frippery," he replied in an amused, quiet tone and retreated back behind his newspaper. He seemed in no hurry to head to his office at the Golden Star Oil Company, most likely because he wanted to surreptitiously hear all about their evening.

"Even so, I'm not sure it was the best decision, dear," Eula said as she dropped her crumbled biscuit onto a waiting Limoges bread plate. "I know Annie pressured you and you of course went along to keep her in line, but a speakeasy? You're both so young and pretty. Surely the dances at the club are much more enjoyable and, well, *civilized*."

Aunt Eula hadn't spent much time in the shrubbery outside the club or inspecting the backseats of parked cars in the lot on dance nights if she thought country club boys behaved any better than the fellows she'd seen at the speak the night before. She wondered for a brief moment if Mac Adair would take such liberties, then chided herself. Of course he would, and at every opportunity. That sardonic expression and handsome demeanor would cut a wide swath through most of the feminine population of any location.

"We had no difficulties with anyone," Lilly assured the older woman even as she regretted her small deception. Annie, Walter, and Ray hadn't had any problems. They'd drunk and laughed and danced as they were supposed to. Only Lilly had encountered a fly in the proverbial ointment, which was ironic considering she'd been the only sober one there.

Aunt Eula nodded and shifted some of the creamed beef around on her plate. Rather than take a bite, she returned her soft, blue-eyed gaze to Lilly. "Tell me, what was it like?"

Uncle Wendell's paper rattled again and Eula frowned at her husband. "Come now, you're curious too, Mr. Beechly. Unless you've already been there with your compatriots from the oil company, carousing and imbibing."

He said nothing and Eula dismissed him with a dip of her chin. "Tell me, were the women dressed indecently?"

Lilly took her time answering as she wished Annie was here to provide colorful commentary rather than sleeping late and avoiding the inquisition. "I didn't see any indecent clothing. Some poor color choices, but nothing terribly shocking." Not shocking in the context of a speakeasy. She knew her aunt would have been aghast at the display of exposed garters and rouged knees.

"That's a relief. What about the company? Was it *mixed*?" Eula's eyes widened as she contemplated the idea. Her aunt had come from conservative stock and she drew great comfort in knowing the proper places for everyone and everything in society from where the fingerbowls should be placed, to who should marry. Thus her distress over her daughter's rebellious ways, and her perplexed attitude towards Lilly's reforming social platforms. Aunt Eula was too polite to argue about it, but made it clear she had no intention of voting in future elections. Lilly had known better than to ever mention some of her more radical ideas to the older woman.

"No." There was no way she'd mention the racial makeup of most of the band members since they weren't technically patrons of the speak but more hired help. If she did, Annie would be firmly restricted to home for the remainder of the summer, and Lilly might be politely loaded on the interurban to return to the farm. At least

Mrs. Crumrine's information hadn't been that explicit. Lilly missed the quiet of the farm but had no intention of going home just yet. There was still too much to see and do in town.

"I'm sure Walter and Ray kept you both safe. Both such nice boys from good families." Aunt Eula's voice took on a wistful quality and Lilly prepared herself for some gentle hints about getting serious, setting a date, and how lovely autumn weddings could be. Before her aunt could launch into pleasant daydreams about golden chrysanthemum floral arrangements leaving her with nothing more to do than nod and scoop thick, floury gravy into mounds on her plate, thumping and rustling sounds interrupted. All three of them looked up to find Annie leaning on the breakfast room door frame. She slouched in rumpled emerald silk pajamas, her short hair in disarray as she blinked shadowed eyes at her mother, father, and finally Lilly.

"Hey, all," she drawled as she slumped into the room to take her seat at the table. Aunt Eula's lips drew into a thin line as she watched her daughter listlessly serve herself some breakfast. Annie's lips curled as she looked over the repulsive offerings and Lilly felt a stab of sympathy for her hung-over cousin. Uncle Wendell went so far as to lower his paper to get a look.

"What do you have to say for yourself, missy?" Eula tut-tutted as she poured Annie a cup of coffee.

"Not much." Annie turned her head slowly and fixed bloodshot eyes on Lilly.

"They know." Lilly whispered.

"Did you tell?" Annie hissed back, her gray face going another shade paler.

"She didn't have to say a word. Everyone and his cousin saw you there, and the worst gossips on Market Street are jamming the phone lines with their evil speculations." Eula's tone had taken on the sorrow of a shamed mother as she wearily stirred her coffee with a sterling spoon.

"Now, Mrs. Beechly. No harm done." Wendell made a show of folding his paper before he settled it on the embroidered tablecloth. "I'm sure both our girls behaved themselves while managing to have an exciting evening."

Lilly felt her cheeks warm as shivers of embarrassment clenched her belly. She hadn't behaved herself, at least not to the standards she set. Certainly not whenever she'd been knee to knee with Mac Adair.

"And it's not as if any of us refrain from gossip." Uncle Wendell cocked a bushy eyebrow at Aunt Eula and rose from his seat with a grunt. He straightened his pinstripe vest over his belly, adjusted his heavy watch chain, and gathered his jacket from the back of the chair. He kissed his wife and daughter's cheeks, and left Lilly with a buss on her head as he went on his way to keep the world moving forward with oil-refining profits.

"I don't gossip," Eula defended herself as soon as her husband was out of earshot.

"Mother. Please." Annie shook her head with impatience, winced, and reached for her coffee. "All you could talk about yesterday morning was who the new neighbors might be."

Lilly's ears pricked up at this. So the old Newell place finally had residents. It was about time. The imposing brick house next door had been vacant for over a year after the last Newell had fled Ohio winters for a permanent residence in a Florida citrus orchard.

"It was hard not to notice all those men wandering in and out carrying furniture. Perspiring." Aunt Eula's eyebrows went up as the corners of her mouth turned down.

"I missed the furniture. And the sweaty men. What did you see?" Annie urged her mother to move on to a new topic far removed from the previous evening's entertainments. Lilly tapped her foot against her cousin's leg to let her know she was onto the distraction.

"Not very much. A few crates and a large mattress but no frame or headboard. Nothing that looked like it belonged to children."

"Perhaps more will be delivered later." Lilly smiled at the thought of children moving in. She could invite them over for hot cocoa in the winter, perhaps take them to the Farout Park zoo later this summer. They might distract her from her own lack. She and Daniel had so wanted children. When he'd died, Lilly's grief ballooned to unbearable when she found out a week later she hadn't conceived yet again.

She impaled a piece of pineapple and watched the syrup drip back into the bowl. It was the middle of summer and there were fresh strawberries, raspberries, and cherries in the market but Mrs. Kessler merely opened a tin and dumped the contents into a bowl. She doubted the housekeeper had even looked at the label first. It was at times like this Lilly missed having control of her own kitchen and access to hedgerows filled with berry bushes.

"Oh, but I did see a Frigidaire delivery van. Whatever it was, it was well-crated and very heavy. It took all the men to lift it up the steps. It seemed to be quite a strain." Aunt Eula lifted one eyebrow as she dropped this bombshell.

"Really?" Lilly gushed, thrilled at the idea of a refrigerator so nearby. She'd wanted one for several years, but her late husband had always claimed construction of a separate power plant was too expensive and an icebox would do. "I wonder if it has a freezer tray?"

"Maybe we'll get lucky and be invited over to sample an ice cube in July," Annie murmured. "Did you see the owner, Mama?"

Eula tilted her head to the side. "I don't know. It was just several large men in and out a few times so perhaps the owners will show up today."

"I saw a light on early this morning, so someone was staying there. I was afraid it was a ghost. That house had always given me the heebie-jeebies." Annie pushed away from her plate and swallowed a few times. Lilly had heard about the aftereffects of overindulgence and she hoped Annie wasn't going to experience a bout of nausea all over the Aubusson rug.

"Of course, you saw a light early this morning, since you were out until then doing heaven knows what." Mrs. Kessler had crept in unnoticed and looked over the still laden breakfast table with a pursed mouth. Lilly couldn't resist narrowing her own lips in response. "It's no wonder you aren't eating, considering what you've been up to."

Aunt Eula pretended not to hear the impertinence as she rose and placed her napkin on the table. "Mrs. Kessler, do you know if our new neighbors have hired help yet? Perhaps you might consider anyone of your acquaintance who might be in search of employment."

Shaking her head at the idea that more employees of their housekeeper's ilk might soon be taking up residence next door, Lilly decided she'd try to be neighborly and make a few recommendations first. If she brought over a welcoming dish, it might ease the way for the newcomers.

"Aunt Eula, if you don't mind, I'd like to bake a pie and take it over this afternoon. Welcome whoever is living there and offer any assistance we might render."

"That's a wonderful idea, Lilly. Very charitable." Aunt Eula beamed at her before turning her mouth down at her own daughter, who seemed to have missed most of the conversation as she sipped a glass of water with great concentration. Lilly kept a wary eye on the suffering young woman. This might just be the lesson that cured Annie of her enthusiasm for liquor.

She waited for her aunt to leave the breakfast room before speaking to the housekeeper. The older woman breathed heavily and gave short, aggrieved shakes of her head. "What sort of fresh fruit do we have in the pantry, Mrs. Kessler?"

The housekeeper stacked plates with a clatter as she cleared the table. Lilly had tried to assist the first morning she'd been there, but had been swiftly reprimanded. "None. Angelo hasn't been by yet this morning and what he had on his wagon yesterday wasn't nice quality. Don't know why Mrs. Beechly insists on dealing with that Italian when there's a perfectly good American-run store a few blocks away."

"It must be her sense of Christian charity." Lilly put on her sweetest smile, the one she used when old men scoffed at her. Angelo Ciminillo sold beautiful produce from his humble wagon. It was far more likely Mrs. Kessler hadn't wanted to go to the trouble of selecting anything and prepare it later. In any case, it made Lilly's morning easier. She'd go to the closest diner and have an edible breakfast and on her walk home she'd keep a lookout for Angelo.

## Chapter Four

Annie was napping and Aunt Eula had left the house to visit a friend from church who was feeling poorly, so Lilly made her solitary way over to the old Newell house as she balanced a still-warm strawberry rhubarb pie on her hands. Mrs. Kessler had glowered at her and made disparaging comments the whole time Lilly worked in the kitchen, but the pastry turned out perfectly flaky and the filling had just the right balance of tart and sweet. It was the sort of treat folks deserved after spending an exhausting day amongst the chaos of moving.

The lawn between the Beechly home and the newly-occupied house took only a moment for her to navigate. She'd considered walking all the way down her front sidewalk and then back up the neighbor's but rejected it as too formal. If they were going to live so near each other, treading a bit on their overgrown grass seemed acceptable.

Huge elm trees arched overhead, blocking most of the bright afternoon sun. She glanced up at the ornate brick façade of the Newell house. She'd always liked the looming tower section. Her imagination had made it the backdrop of every romantic story she'd read when she was a girl. She'd often stayed in town with her aunt and uncle when her own mother had been melancholy and Lilly had sat in her bedroom and stared across at rough stone blocks and leaded windows as she daydreamed. The Newells had been reclusive and she'd never been given a chance to see the interior of the imposing house, and certainly never the tower. Perhaps the new owners were more social and she might be invited up some time.

Making her way up the wide stone steps to the porch, she shifted the pie to one hand and pressed the doorbell with the other. There was a barely discernible chime through the leaded glass and walnut door but no other sound. Lilly waited and pressed the button again. There might not be anyone home. Perhaps the family was out shopping for furniture together, or at their previous residence packing last minute items. Casting around the bare porch for something to set the pie on, Lilly noticed movement behind the facets of glass in the door window but still jumped when the door opened with a rattle and creak.

When she recognized the person glaring at her, all the breath left her body in a gasp and her knees went weak. It was Mac Adair. Of course. Of all the people in Lima who could have purchased the house next to hers, it would have to be that man.

He narrowed his eyes at her and propped his arm across the door opening as if to deny her entrance. Rather than hold his gaze, Lilly let her eyes rove elsewhere. He was wearing a soft-looking red shirt with far too many buttons unfastened, and sturdy black trousers. When she realized he wasn't wearing an undershirt and she could see the tan skin tight against the muscles of his chest, her arms weakened and the pie wobbled and dropped from her useless hands.

Stifling a shriek, Lilly flailed for the pan but it was too late to catch it. Spraying its contents, the pie landed on the porch with a sickening squash and the entire pastry top cracked apart as reddish goo welled up like heart's blood. Scarlet gobbets clung to her forearms and the front of her embroidered linen dress.

Horrified, she looked up to find Mac Adair still staring at her, although his features had smoothed away from the frown he'd worn earlier. The corners of his mouth twitched with disgust or amusement at her predicament. Lilly knew her own mouth was gaping open but she was frozen with embarrassment and powerless to close it.

\*\*\*\*

Stricken might be too strong a word for Mac to apply in this circumstance, but it came damn close. Perhaps another might find humor in this beauty brought to her knees by some version of slapstick, but he was mortified for her.

It wasn't lost on him, this neighborly gesture of welcome, although no doubt she'd have painted a black daub on his door to warn others had she known he lived here after the way he'd treated her in his speakeasy, although she'd given as good as she'd got. The very shock of his appearance causing her to drop the offering of what smelled like a mighty fine fruit pie, the aromas of tart rhubarb, sugar and spice wafting up to entice his senses, spoke to her unawareness of the identity of her new neighbor. An entirely inappropriate thought wound its way through his mind as he considered how such a succulent mixture might taste if devoured from her creamy skin—Mac stopped that fantasy dead in its tracks and fumbled for his handkerchief.

"Here, let me…" He squatted to reach out and pat the worst of the spill from her wrist then thought better of it and offered the cloth to her to apply instead.

Trembling fingers snatched it from his grasp, the slight contact sparking a frission of static up his forearm. Lil patted at each patch of sticky fruit and flakes of pastry while avoiding his eyes, not a word passing her lips, closed now into a thin line as she visibly regained her composure. Not that her full, bee-stung mouth could compress into a truly regimented grimace. He filled the silence by making ineffectual attempts to gather the

47

remaining sludge from the floor boards of the porch onto the pie plate.

"Thank you." A quiet, dignified murmur at last. She raised her coffee brown eyes to his again, the long lashes sweeping up to unveil returning self possession. The dichotomy of this woman made his heart pound harder, and another part of his anatomy responded as well, refusing to listen to his brain scold.

As awkward as a boy in the company of his first crush, Mac struggled to his feet, offering her the hand not occupied with the detritus of the pie as he did so. Lil reached out to take it, and their fingers met amidst the gooey residue as he helped her up. He felt his lips twitching and registered a similar movement of Lil's. Laughter bubbled over, a welcome warmth that enveloped his senses, and he guffawed in response.

"Mac Adair."

"Lilly Townsend."

"My pleasure to meet you, Miss Townsend. Please come in and you can freshen up."

Her delectable nose twitched and she gestured at her person with a wry grimace. "I think it will take more than a mere *freshen up*. And it's Mrs. Townsend, but please call me Lilly. After our two, um, disparate meetings…"

He barely registered her attempt at referring to last night's emotionally charged introduction. *She was married? How had he missed that fine gold band? Married to that sap.*

"Ah—" What in hell was that man's name? He had it—at least his first name. "So, Walter is your husband."

"Walter? Heavens, no! My husband passed four years ago."

The rush of relief at the news made his knees weak—he was a total bastard for welcoming such news—and he fought against the totally unfamiliar feeling and forced his tongue to become unstuck and say the words he really didn't mean. "I'm sorry for your loss, Lilly."

"Thank you." She stared at him expectantly and he shuffled backwards into the foyer. Lilly gracefully followed, only to come up short. She cast a glance back over her shoulder, and he watched as hectic color bloomed on her cheekbones.

"I shouldn't. I mean … the neighbors … is there anyone else in the house?"

"Just me, Lilly." Mac understood her anxiety. No woman of good reputation would compromise herself by entering a house occupied solely by a man, and likely not even if there was a maid or housekeeper present. Appearances still counted for a lot. He knew he should encourage her to leave, but a very selfish part of him refused.

Indecisiveness warred with some other emotion on her lovely face—he thought it might be rebellion, although it stood to reason that a well-mannered woman wouldn't be rebellious. He waited with bated breath for her decision.

"Do you have a powder room on the main floor?"

"There's a newly constructed bath just off the foyer." He nodded in the direction.

With a firm nod of her pointed chin she squared her shoulders and marched that way. He wondered if she visualized it as a journey into perdition. Shaking his head, he stepped out onto the porch to scan the surroundings, taking a quick glance up and down the street. He didn't see any pedestrians or take note of people lurking behind their lace curtained windows, but the mansions were set well apart so he likely wouldn't see them if they were.

Although they might well have noticed Lilly attending his home.

Carefully disposing of the ruined pie in his sterile kitchen, the new Frigidaire his only nod to the current times, he hustled back to the porch with a rag and a small basin of water. He hadn't cleaned a floor on his knees in, well, ever, but the flies were gathering and there was no way Lil—Lilly—was going to play the washerwoman in full display to their street. He really needed to hire some help.

It wasn't as difficult as he'd imagined. The bulk of the disaster had been absorbed by Lilly's pretty dress, so he'd completed the chore and discarded the evidence before she emerged from the bathroom. He'd changed places in the foyer twice, while awaiting her arrival, shifting from a casual position against the wall between two ostentatious pictures—the salesperson had insisted they were all the rage—to standing at parade rest in the center of the hall. It was an effort not to rock back on his heels as he wracked his brains as to what he might say to her.

From the look on her face, Lilly's sojourn in the bathroom hadn't been spent entirely on cleaning up. While the stuff of her dress sported large, spreading damp spots tinged with an unfortunate hue of pink, a tribute to the tenacity of nature's color palette, the same hint of blush remained on her cheeks. She'd been thinking. At least he surmised she had. Her opening words coined it.

"I had no idea you were my aunt and uncle's new neighbor." The frost was back in her tone, all evidence of the collusion of their humor erased.

"Or you wouldn't have deigned to make me a welcome to the neighborhood pie. Let alone cross the threshold." Damn it, he was biting back as a dog snaps at flies.

She flinched at his comment and held her head even higher. "I definitely wouldn't have. You own a speakeasy! Your reputation—"

Mac cut her off. "*My* reputation? I'm a businessman, Mrs. Townsend. I serve the public, at least those who seek my services. And if memory serves, you were in my speak just last night. How might that have impugned your reputation, I wonder? Or perhaps it reflected who you are beneath the trappings."

If he could have ripped out his tongue by its very roots he would have done. What had happened to that slight meeting of the minds on his doorstep? He could admit he'd hoped they'd moved on past last night. Lilly's breasts lifted and fell rapidly in response to his set down and he tore his eyes away from that bewitching sight to meet her very hurt gaze, swiftly being hidden by outrage and disdain.

"*I* know who I am beneath my *trappings*. Mr. Adair. Who or what do you hide behind yours? My slight lapse in judgment last evening, correction, serious lapse in judgment won't be repeated. Of that I can assure you!"

Hell's teeth, she was lovely! All flashing eyes and high color. He couldn't resist pushing her harder, knowing it was the result of considerable disappointment. Her opinion shouldn't have mattered to him. It wasn't like he was ashamed of what he did, well, a little ashamed. Nonsense.

"I knew my first impression of you was correct, Mrs. Grundy."

She sputtered. It was fascinating to observe, those succulent lips parting with fury before she snapped them shut, drawing in deep breaths through that sweet little nose. He fancied he could hear the thoughts tumbling in her head.

"If you consider calling me priggish and straight-laced an insult, sir, you're sorely mistaken. I'm simply fine with your assessment. At least I'm contributing to the moral compass of this world, unlike some people who undermine the very fabric of—oomph."

Mac wouldn't have been able to explain why he did what he did, not then or later. But it was just too much. Too much of everything. She had slipped a verbal dagger between his ribs and pierced his conscience, shrouded as it was by the flow of cash and his continual repetition of how he was simply giving the public—the wealthy public—what it wanted. Coupled with her intense appeal, he felt pushed over the brink and reacted to both quiet her and soothe his abraded soul.

Her wealth of hair spilled from its gathered twist on the back of her head as he pulled her roughly into his arms, soft curves imprinting against his chest. He caught a glimpse of her wide, startled eyes before taking her mouth with his own in fierce possession. She tasted of mint and fruit. He wondered if she'd tasted her own baking, before plundering the seam of her lips and ravishing the heat beneath. Groaning with the effort of suppressing his lust—he longed to sweep her up and carry her into the parlor where a fainting couch reposed—Mac contented himself with kissing them both senseless.

Lilly's body relaxed from its stiff stance as she melted into his embrace, her hips now flush with his own. He could feel the slender strength beneath her pliant form and wrapped her closer, tightening the cage of his arms while sliding a hand to cup her skull, fingers wreathing through the soft strands of her hair. As he reluctantly lifted his head to allow them both the opportunity to breathe, her lids flickered open, her lashes the flutter of tiny bird wings. He fell into the brilliance of her unfocused, velvety brown eyes, knowing the wonder of what just transpired was mirrored in his own.

Even as he drank in the sight of her wide-eyed gaze and trembling, swollen lips, the part of Lilly he'd scornfully referred to as Mrs. Grundy resurfaced. Her mouth firmed and her hands jerked from their tense hold on his shoulders to insinuate themselves between them. An abrupt push, accompanied by a shift of her weight, and he accommodatingly relaxed his hold to release her. It killed him to let her go but he did it. If a hint of fear had invaded those gorgeous orbs, well, he would have felt the worst possible heel.

Fingers immediately worrying the strands of her released hair, Lilly gave him her back while she forced the shining stuff into some semblance of order with the few pins that hadn't pinged to the floor, a musical accompaniment to that kiss. Mac stooped and busied himself with picking up those that were within reach—it served to calm his arousal and took his mind off of how Lilly would look with her arms raised, presenting the swell of her breast to his avid gaze. He absorbed the view as he straightened to his feet, his eyes sweeping the length of her legs, swelling calves above nicely turned ankles, followed by a sweetly curved backside.

She caught him staring as she turned to face him once again and flashed him an annoyed look. Solemnly he offered the hair accessories and she nearly snatched them off his palm, driving them home with aggravated movements and granting him his wish. The curves beneath her dress lifted and he caught the faint jut of her softening nipples behind the still damp linen, blinking against the memory of those far harder points against his chest moments earlier.

Should he apologize? She saved him the trouble of deciding. "You, sir, slay me."

"Slang, Mrs. Townsend?"

"Hardly, Mr. Adair. What … what just happened was hardly humorous."

"Not in the least," he agreed, gravely.

Lilly blinked at him. "Who are you, sir?"

"I might ask you the same thing, madam."

"We appear to bring out the worst in one another," she allowed.

"If that kiss was the worst, Mrs. Townsend, then I look forward to the best."

Her face flamed and breath soughed in and out of her luscious chest. "That won't happen again."

"Pity. I thought it was unreal." It was his turn to use the current slang. But it *had* been special and something told him not to allow her to minimize it.

"I pride myself on being honest, Mr. Adair. I allow the kiss was … unreal… but I'm—"

"What? A married woman instead of a widow? A temperance leader? "

Her eyes shifted and she looked at the floor. Damn. He was all balled up, and confusion was the least of it. Was she not a widow? He'd never poach. He had too much pride, and considering his business, if Lilly was against alcohol…

Lilly's head came back up. He was coming to recognize that tilt. "I'm indeed a widow, sir."

Being punched right in the midriff might compare—or not. His brain celebrated her confirmed single status even as it painted the disparity of their situation in life. All his life he'd been given the short end of the stick, the crumbs. He'd clawed his way out of poverty and assumed the mantle of a wealthy, if unscrupulous, businessman, welcome in society, if not in the most polite. He had his pick of women by dint of his business and who had drawn his eye—and other parts of his anatomy.

"You support temperance." No wonder she had refused to drink in his speak.

"And the rights of women. And all those oppressed. I'm passionate about my causes."

The latter should have eased his pain a trifle. Mac knew oppression. But he'd never tell a do-gooder about his past or the fact he hid his Shawnee heritage. Ending up as one of Lilly's causes might have a certain appeal, considering the taste he'd just had of her passion, but it was out of the question. She'd pity him and that he couldn't abide.

Nodding, he eased past her and opened the door. "Thank you for making the attempt to welcome me to the neighborhood. I appreciate it, Mrs. Townsend." Damned if he was going to apologize for that kiss but he wasn't going to refer to it again either.

"Oh. I thought you might wish to pursue our conversation. I have reasons for my beliefs and—"

The combination of shock at her "beliefs" and unsatisfied need made him short with her. "I doubt there is anything further to discuss, Mrs. Townsend. And it's best you depart before anyone who noticed your visit begins to mark the time. Reputation and all. No matter if half the people living on this street have been to my establishment," he concluded grimly.

He'd hurt her again, offended her. Mac thought it odd he could read this Lilly Townsend so well, so early in their association. Association? They were neighbors was all. And ones who'd ignore one another for perpetuity. Hardening his heart, he ensured she had plenty of room to pass him as she exited his home. Grasping the door handle firmly kept him from laying that hand on her, although he shoved his free one into his pocket to be sure. That tempting curve of her backside…

"Good day, Mrs. Townsend."

"Goodbye, Mr. Adair." Her farewell sounded as though gritted through every last one of her little, white teeth.

He didn't allow himself to watch her descend the steps, closing the heavy wooden panels quietly behind her, the leaded glass warping his last visual. A heavy feeling compressed his chest and shoulders as he turned and made his way to fix a pot of coffee and some breakfast. The memory of the pie mocked him. She'd tasted sweeter than pie and *that* memory stirred parts of him barely subsiding in her absence.

## Chapter Five

Lilly had heard enough giggling to last her the rest of the day. Her head ached and her cheeks hurt from all the polite smiles she'd had to give during the bridal tea festivities. She was seated at a long table covered with pale blue cloth in the lunch room of the Shawnee Country Club while surrounded by a host of other young women, all squealing with excitement over Miss Flora Robertson's upcoming wedding to one of the Baxter brothers. She wasn't sure which Baxter was tying the knot. There were four of them, each born a year apart and all sharing the family traits of thick brown hair and soulful dark eyes. They had made their way through the young women of Lilly's set but it seemed one of them was settling down with the pale, plump, and shy Flora. At least the cake had been cut and served which meant the end of the event was in sight.

Her neighbors chattered about silver patterns and where to find the best stockings in town, but Lilly stayed quiet and stared at the floral arrangement of white sweetheart roses in front of her. Somehow being at this bridal shower put her in a melancholy frame of mind today. She'd been through many since her husband's death, and had finally stopped feeling a pang of grief whenever she thought of her wedding day or of her loss whenever an excited bride-to-be showed an engagement ring or walked down the aisle in her finery. But today was different.

Hoping she wasn't falling prey to her mother's affliction of perpetual melancholia, Lilly shook her head and glanced out the sparkling windows with a splendid view of the manicured lawns and golf course of the club. Men in knickers and vests moved at a leisurely pace as they played. Everything was as it should be; clean, understated, and separate from the strain and dirt of real life. Like marriages became after the gifts were opened and the dress was packed in camphor.

"What's it like, Lilly?" Peg Finley's question interrupted her maudlin thoughts and Lilly turned to face the smiling young woman. She hoped this wasn't another request for information about what happened in the marriage bed. Every event of this sort she'd attended included a few inquiries along those lines and she did her best to be encouraging and discreet, but today, with the lurking memory of Mac's burning kiss and strong hands, it was close to unbearable.

"What's what like?" She'd lost track of the conversation while reminiscing about that man's tongue touching her own. The whole encounter had been simply unbelievable.

"Why, that speakeasy on the south side near the Locomotive Works. How's the 'tea' there?" The young woman hissed out the euphemism for liquor like she was uttering a curse word in church.

Vera Longworth, Lilly's neighbor on the other side of the table, cut into the conversation as she leaned close to the tabletop to catch Lilly's gaze. "Don't be silly, Peggy, Lilly's not a drinker."

"It's not just drinking." Peggy regrouped and adjusted the long line of blue Venetian beads around her neck. "They have dancing and bands. Both George Cooper and Bill Wilton were there just last night and told me all about it. There was a *colored* band, they claimed."

"What makes you think I've been there?" Lilly couldn't help herself from asking as she wondered what epic gossip Mrs. Crumrine might have been spreading all over town. Her whole body chilled and tensed when she thought of what the elder woman would have said if she'd spied Mac Adair and the horrible scene Lilly had experienced with him the previous afternoon. Her humiliation had been complete, from the mess of the poor, ruined pie to the incredible spectacle she'd made of herself in his arms. In his arms! She'd never behaved in such a debauched manner before and thinking of it made her head hurt even worse. An ache spread from her tight throat to her chest as she commanded herself to stop thinking about how he'd tasted of cinnamon and how her knees had wobbled after only a second of his touch.

"Why, Annie told me, of course." Vera raised her eyebrows like it should be obvious. "My advice is to go there soon before they shut it down."

"Shut it down? Why? Who?" Peggy sounded like she'd never heard of the Volstead Act. Maybe she hadn't, considering her life-long aversion to reading.

"The police and Treasury Department agents," Lilly explained. She felt a tickle of worry as she contemplated what might happen to Mac. He was so confident and self-assured, but how would that help him when they arrested him and threw him in a dank jail cell? They'd probably rough him up if he argued with them as he had with her. Strike his face, black one of his gleaming eyes, bruise his tender mouth…

"They'll have to stand in line." Vera took a petite sip of her tea and curled her pink lips into a knowing grin.

"Behind who?" Lilly was digging for information now, the vision of a battered and bleeding Mac helpless on a hard cell cot swimming in her vision.

"The Knights, of course. They're hardly going to stand for such a place in our city. It represents everything they fight against. And, if they knew there was a colored band in the place last night, it would be demolished by tomorrow."

Lilly tried not to look as uneasy as she felt. Instead, she picked up her teacup and took a swallow of the tepid liquid. Despite how much she was shaking, it barely rattled leaving the saucer. Her mouth had gone dry, and her belly fluttered along with her heartbeats. The Klan was a terrifying thought. Mac's fate with them would involve burning crosses on the lawn and him hanging from a nearby tree. Her stomach rolled and she wished she hadn't eaten the cucumber sandwiches.

"What about the owner?" Trust Peggy to ask.

Lilly's lips trembled as she remembered his kiss. No, *their* kiss, she'd been a willing participant and shouldn't pretend to be an overwhelmed female. Unreal, he'd called it. He probably said that to every woman he kissed so skillfully, which was almost certainly a huge number. She found herself short of breath, so she stared at the sliver of white cake on a white plate in front of her and tried to refocus.

"He's quite the mystery." Vera leaned even closer to the table to whisper, the petals of a rose touching her cheek as her eyes glittered with excitement. "Rich, handsome, and an utter scoundrel. The bee's knees of bootleggers."

"Is he from Chicago?" Peggy's eyes were wide as she considered it.

Vera shook her head and squinted her eyes. "Who knows? He has to be a gangster. He probably carries a gun and has henchmen at his beck and call."

Peggy let out a tiny squeal and Lilly gulped. Had she pressed herself so intimately against a hardened criminal? Was Mr. Adair the sort of man who'd beat his enemies? Would he abuse women and corrupt the police in pursuit of profit? Her previously upset stomach clenched tighter and she plotted the course to the restroom, just in case.

"Really? Why don't the police stop him?" Peggy's pale eyes were nearly bulging out of her head and Lilly wondered if she was going to suffer brain fever.

"Because they're hampered by politicians and public opinion. That's why the Knights are probably going to take steps. It's something our men will have to take into their own hands. You know, my brothers are in the Knights, and they come home from their little meetings full of fire and talk. It's very entertaining."

Lilly wasn't sure how a person could find lynchings, anti-Semitism, and xenophobia entertaining. She felt sick when she thought about it and horrified that people she knew, and had shared a table with, were members. She'd grown up with the idea it was a Southern problem, hidden in rural areas and isolated towns, but the Klan had grown in size and visibility in the last few years. She'd known the Longworth boys since they were children and learning they were members made her dizzy.

"So what are they going to do?" Peggy sampled a bite of cake and now sounded as collected as if she was asking about what activities would be on offer at the next lawn fete. Lilly almost bent her teaspoon in disgust and fear. Fear of Mac. Fear for Mac. Did he know he was a target?

"Who knows? Right now they're mad about how dodgy things have gotten in Snaketown. They say decent women shouldn't walk in that neighborhood even in the middle of the day. The hooligans have gotten that bold."

Someone called her name and Lilly broke away from the fascinating and revolting discussion. Annie stood in the wide doorway of the lunchroom, waving at the women who called out greetings to her as she gestured with her chin for Lilly to come to her. She was wearing a bright blue day dress, and her eyes gleamed with the determined expression Lilly knew all too well.

Excusing herself from the table and giving Vera Longworth the same wary consideration she'd give a coiled snake, Lilly walked over to Annie who promptly turned away and went toward the library room. As soon as she entered, her cousin closed the door behind them and drew Lilly down to a velvet sofa. Annie peered around the deserted and shaded room smelling of cigars and held a finger up to her lips.

"Why all the secrecy?"

"I need your help, Lil."

Lilly looked over her cousin and sighed. Not again. "What is it?" *This time*.

"I need you to come out with me tonight."

Lilly shook her head, remembering Aunt Eula's firm commandment that her daughter needed to stay in the remainder of the week, as a punishment for going to the speakeasy. Lilly had been happy to hear the prohibition. It meant there would be no possibility she'd encounter that man again. She might get lucky. With the hours he must keep, running his infernal den, their paths might not cross for months.

Annie pursed her rouged lips together and leaned forward. "Come on, Lilibet. It's just for a little while, so I can talk to Ray."

"Use the telephone."

"I can't, there's no privacy on the line, or at our house or his. We had a fight and I need to make it up to him. I need to see him to, ah, apologize, or he'll meet some hotsy-totsy and drop me like yesterday's news." The burden of impending singlehood toppled Annie over into the down-filled seat cushions and she moaned with anguish. Her dress rode up over her knees and Lilly resisted her urge to pull the hem down.

Dear Lord, how was she planning to appease Raymond? Surely not with *that*. With a rush of warmth over her skin, Lilly remembered how Mac's touch had made her legs quiver and her breath catch. She'd been ready to appease him, or let him appease her in any way he might have suggested. Something in his sure touch and confident manner told Lilly he wouldn't be the diffident lover her late husband had been. Did that make her a hypocrite?

"See him at church tomorrow." Lilly knew this suggestion was almost cruel. Annie hated to go to church and the young couple wouldn't have any privacy there at all, but perhaps that was for the best under the circumstances.

"Lilly! Don't be ridiculous. Just come out with me tonight. I promise I won't need more than ten minutes to see him and then we can go right home. I'll be happy, Ray'll be happy, and you'll be happy. Because I'm happy!" Annie's winsome smile made Lilly want to roll her eyes.

Shaking her head at her cousin's dramatic prediction, Lilly wanted to set a good example for Annie. She always had. When she'd been Annie's age, she'd already married, sent her husband off to war, and welcomed him back. Less than a year later, she'd become a widow. Lilly wasn't sure she'd ever thrown herself on a sofa with such agony over any of it.

Aunt Eula and Uncle Wendell insisted their only daughter simply felt things more deeply than others. Lilly had always suspected Annie instead wanted to cause grand emotion in others. Once when they'd been young girls, Annie had decided to play Rapunzel which had put Lilly in the position of suitor climbing up a rope to her window. Lilly had fallen and cut her head on a stone, but it was Annie's inconsolable hysteria which had prompted a call for the doctor.

"Nothing about going to that place again would make me happy. And besides, how do you know he'll be there?"

"Because it's what we fought about, or at least part of it. He said he was going even if I couldn't and I thought it horribly selfish of him."

Lilly wracked her brain for a way to abide by Eula's dictate and still help her cousin's social life. There was no way she was placing herself within ten feet of Mac Adair, not when she was still warm from his embrace. She and Annie could go somewhere at supper time, meet Ray, and be back before it was technically evening. "How about this? You call Ray and ask him to meet us at the Lima Driving Park for a picnic and I'll take a walk on the grounds while you talk. If we're back before dark I doubt your mother will mind at all."

"That won't work. He'll still go to the club later without me."

"It's the best I can do. Invite him to the house to listen to the radio tonight if you're worried about where he's going."

Another groan from Annie as she reclined on the sofa was the only response Lilly heard. The doors to the library rattled open and two older gentlemen tottered in clutching cigars and newspapers. Quite the fire hazard. Lilly reached out and pulled down Annie's skirt before either of their rheumy eyes caught a glimpse of anything untoward.

## Chapter Six

Snarling at his employees was out of character and he well knew it. They were working at full capacity, even the clean-up man Mac suspected slept in the storage room at every opportunity and reeked of illicit nips from the whiskey barrel. He was pushing his broom with alacrity while avoiding Mac's furious stare. Mac tore his eyes away and tried to settle his innards. What on earth was wrong with him? *Lilly Townsend is what's wrong with you. That "butter wouldn't melt in her mouth" Mrs. Grundy who just happens to live next door.*

More disgruntled at his thoughts than anything else, he shoved away from the bar and climbed the stairs to his office, knowing they were all casting speculative looks behind his back. Lilly wasn't like that. Butter would definitely melt. That kiss melted *him*, and despite their harsh parting words, and his determination not to think about her, he desperately wanted to spoon with Lilly again. And a whole lot more. Gentlemen weren't supposed to have such carnal thoughts and he wondered who had ever come up with that ridiculous notion. All men had carnal thoughts, and the ribald talk and behavior in this very speak, night after night, underscored the fact.

Except he had more than carnal thoughts about Lilly Townsend. She wasn't a cheap floozie. She had integrity and intelligence beneath a very pleasing exterior, and if she was feisty and opinionated, well, witness how all the other women in his life had bored him to tears outside the bedroom. She impressed him as being a total woman, someone any man would be lucky to woo and win. He threw himself into his chair and tipped his head back, studying the tin ceiling. Hadn't he told himself she wasn't for the likes of him?

He'd have to be content merely thinking about her, savoring the memory of that impetuous but oh-so-earth shattering kiss, and pretending she didn't live right next door. So near … and yet so unattainable. He straightened and yanked a pile of invoices toward him. The speak would open shortly and he had a mountain of paperwork to complete. There were other things to deal with as well. The cops were quiet for the time being, but disconcerting rumors of the local Klan were circulating among those in his employ who paid close attention to such things.

Mac briefly considered dismissing his colored band until things quieted. The Knights could get all fueled up on rotgut and talk themselves into upholding the law and "cleaning up" the city. But the members of the orchestra needed the work, not to mention bringing in his customers. He shook his head and concentrated on the task at hand. He'd think on that issue later.

Crowd noise heightened his focus as he worked to reconcile last month's orders with the expenses. The speak was doing well—very well. He needed to find other places to invest the proceeds in the event things went south, and decided to find the time on the morrow to visit the rail line offices and observe for himself how well that particular venture was doing. Perhaps he'd buy there. The stock market wasn't his favorite purview but he couldn't store all his proceeds in the bank, or his mattress. Fertile land was always a good investment. Once again shards of memory from his poverty stricken past infiltrated his mind. Little John hadn't had a mattress, sharing a pallet of straw covered in a filthy piece of cloth his mother had likely rescued from a burn pile somewhere.

A knock at the door fortunately interrupted his thoughts.

"Sir?" Phillip was rubbing his hands together, a sure sign of anxiety.

"What's going on?"

"We're at full capacity tonight, sir. And there's a crowd at the door."

He considered quickly. "Have a couple of the servers and Joseph push some of the barrels and crates to one side of the store room. That bleached linen, the bolts that were mistakenly included in last month's shipment—pull out as much yardage as you need to drape that side of the room off, and dust the chairs out back. Use some barrels for tables."

"Barrels?" Phillip seriously had no imagination.

"We have no other tables. Put candles in glass jars and cut some more linen to cover the barrels. Then seat people." Lord knew what his patrons would make of their surroundings, but if the liquor flowed and the music was loud enough he suspected they wouldn't really care.

"And Phillip? The first round will be on the house. For everyone." That should divert any raised eyebrows.

The bartender blinked then shuffled off to do his bidding. Mac wondered who'd been manning the bar in his absence. He really counted on Phil and maybe the man needed a promotion of sorts, something where he could move around more freely. Give Mac a chance to—what? Spend less time intent on his business to pursue other things? Like that confoundedly irritating woman? Taking her out to enjoy a candlelit dinner in a respectable place, or maybe just the two of them on a Sunday drive? His body warmed at the thought and hardened in places he had no hope of concealing, so he forced his thoughts elsewhere until he calmed.

Pushing back his chair, he rose to his feet and straightened his apparel, ensuring his stickpin held the folds of his neck piece smoothly in place before shooting his cuffs. The smooth stones of his cuff links reminded him of Lilly's silky—damn it! Yet still his fingertips caressed the surface of the precious stones and his mohair trousers once again belied his tailor's careful fitting. Gritting his teeth he forced a deep breath out his nose and carefully avoided his reflection in the heavily framed looking glass he'd placed to reflect the light from the speak's outer rooms. He knew too well what he would see there.

The high color of arousal would make him look more the savage others thought his people, and in truth, passion and violence elicited a similar countenance. He'd put it to good use in the past to cow his enemies and make those who did business with him think twice about doing him dirty. But rather than unleashing his savage side, Mac wanted nothing more than to track Lilly Townsend down and show her this side of him. Press her up against the nearest hard surface while working one of his hands through that mass of amazing hair to hold her steady for a brutal plunder of those full lips until she breathed for mercy.

How would she taste before he dragged her gown away to reveal the high swell of her breasts? He'd find a tender nub with his lips, and then his teeth, sensually torturing her, allowing her to feel his intense need, his hard shaft pressing against her softness and heat.

Hell and damnation! The abrupt increase in chatter, stomping and clattering of feet and high pitched laughter alerted him to the influx of patrons, effectively ending his fantasy. He couldn't continue on in this vein. He had a business to run and that woman had no place in it or his life. They were as different as chalk and cheese and nothing could ever come of it. He'd find solace elsewhere. No doubt Maisie would be looking for a partner at the end of the night and he could forget his romantic troubles. Romance! His brain was zozzled even if he didn't drink. Lust was the only thing he'd allow to impact his senses and only on his terms.

Striding from the office, down the stairs, and into the depths of the speak, the sudden warmth and varied scents of the close proximity of men and women were nearly overwhelming. He surveyed the premises, feeling more than one look bent on him. The flickering light of the candles from inside the propped open door of the storeroom drew him. He wound his way through the closely clustered tables, nodding and smiling by rote, pressing flesh occasionally as would any politician. He hoped Phillip and the rest of his staff had organized that room while he'd been in his office struggling with the needs of the flesh. And a worrisome tension dead center in his chest.

The cavernous room looked less prepossessing with the barrels and crates swathed in fabric, and some enterprising soul had actually hung some of the stuff in swathes from the ceiling to better veil the actual use of the room. The chairs crowded around the makeshift tables were full, and the small surface of the barrels equally crammed with various tea cups and mugs, some still holding the liquor they camouflaged. The blue of cigarette smoke hued the air. The candlelight assuaged the less ambient electric light and nearly carried the room off as a place for people to comfortably congregate and flout the laws of Prohibition. Mac instantly wondered how he could make this area more appealing in the long run, expand to accommodate those who obviously wanted to patronize his joint.

"Mac!" A cheerful baritone broke into his reverie. He found the source of the voice.

"Hello, Harry."

The local councilman lowered his eye in a vast wink. The man was clearly already lit up like a store window display.

"Was about to cast a kitten when your bruiser on the door told us the place was full. Should have known you'd figure out a way to deal with the crashers! The barrels give the place atmosphere. Alice here says it's like a true speak!"

Alice gave Mac a languid smile, heavily rouged lips quirking in what she probably thought was a come-on, her kohl-lined eyes and clumped eyelashes giving her the look of a sated doper. Nothing like Lilly with her fresh-faced yet classic—*holy hell*. He managed a nod at Alice and shook Harry's hand before trying to take his leave. Alice's ringed hand crept up his outer thigh and he froze. Harry might be low man on the totem pole on council, but he was nobody to mess with. Not to mention he was available for anyone with deep enough pockets to use. Mac didn't want to make an enemy out of the man unnecessarily.

Casually, he stepped back, Alice's fingers slipping away, and he put space between them. Harry was speaking again.

"Might want to look sharp, Mac. The Knights are spoiling for some kind of confrontation." The other man gestured wildly toward the orchestra, the music now swelling above the din. "Those dark folks might make my feet want to jiggle, but we have our standards. Only right, you know."

Was that a thinly veiled warning? Mac stared into the other man's eyes but the booze had disguised any true intent. Alice leaned forward again and he stepped behind the councilman, clapping him on the shoulder in farewell. With unnecessary firmness. The other man's cringe denoted his lack of character. Mac ignored Alice's sultry murmur and headed to the bar to check on the status of the flowing alcohol. If the shrieks of female laughter and rumbles of male mirth were any indication, the free drinks had turned the tide of any dissatisfaction. Mac only hoped the heavy heads and turned stomachs come morning wouldn't dissuade the lot of them from coming back. Unlikely.

A developing ruckus at the entrance to the speakeasy turned his footsteps in that direction. Perhaps his tactics of making more room wasn't enough. Dennis's enormous frame blocked his view, and the upset was somewhat masked by the rousing sounds of a Charleston upswing, but Mac didn't allow dissent in his business. Things got broken, women screamed in terror or excitement and liquor spilled. Not good for business at all.

A raised woman's voice, clearly tearful and distraught, coupled with the deeper base of a less than patient male, filtered to his ears. A domestic. Well, Dennis would have to show them out. Mac moved to lend a hand or distract as the case might be.

"Annie, this is inappropriate! Have a care! There are people you know here."

He wouldn't mistake that voice if he was a hundred years old, blind, deaf and totally in his dotage. And hadn't seen her for the bulk of those years. *Lilly.*

With a word to Dennis, he eased past the bulk of the man and observed a dishevelled young woman—the one he'd seen with Lilly that night he'd first laid eyes on her—hugged tight in Lilly's arms as she spoke words of admonishment and succour into the blonde's ear.

"It'll be fine, Annie. He's... Raymond is merely wishing for some time with his friends."

"That's right, Annie." A tall, well set up man, Annie's escort from the other night, echoed Lilly's sentiments. "I'm not angry any more. I just need time—"

"Time away from me," sobbed Annie, and Mac only just managed not to roll his eyes. Such drama.

"Just give Walter a call, Lilly. He'll be glad to pick you up."

Mac couldn't help but wonder where the young man thought Lilly would find access to a telephone in the middle of the street late at night. Lilly also disliked this advice, judging by the frown that skidded across her face. With an unconcerned shrug, Raymond turned away from the women and gave Dennis a questioning look.

With a gesture from Mac, his door man stepped aside enough to allow Raymond entry, creating a fresh spate of tears and recriminations from Annie. Lilly clasped her tighter and Mac fiercely wished to take the place of the other woman, held close to Lilly's breasts. Lilly looked up and met his gaze.

Mac forgot he was trying to calm a potential disturbance in his business. He forgot there were large numbers of revellers in his speak, the strains of a Lindy Hop now a bizarre backdrop for the pounding of his heart and the pulse of the blood racing through his veins. He wanted Lilly with every fibre of his soul. He stepped into the fray.

"Let me escort you home."

Lilly watched him while Annie sobbed. "Raymond was our transportation," she allowed. "And who knows when he'll be done visiting with his *friends*. I don't suppose you have a telephone in there by any chance?"

Mac shook his head, at ease with his small lie and felt sorry for Raymond when Lilly next made his acquaintance, but he was so pleased to be able to spend time with her again that he dismissed any concern for the other man. Nodding to Dennis brought the other man closer. "Tell Phillip he's to close at our usual time. He's in charge." Dennis's pinched eyes widened a fraction at such unusual behavior but he growled his understanding.

Mac spoke to Lilly. "I'll bring my car around." She nodded solemnly, her attention divided between him and Annie.

\*\*\*\*

Lilly sat with her friend in the crowded back seat of his new Chevrolet. Mac only hoped the engine withstood the trip home, the difficulties with this particular model common across the country. But it delivered them safely, mostly because he somehow kept his eyes on the road and didn't crick his neck stealing glimpses of Lilly. Annie's whimpering made his teeth ache but he admired Lilly's patience with her. She was practical, yet caring and understanding. Something he'd never experienced in his life. Didn't Annie know how lucky she was?

Despite Annie's need for attention, he felt the connection with Lilly, the tension building between them thick and tangible. He pulled the vehicle over in front of his mansion and stopped, applying the handbrake, taking a deep breath and willing his flesh into submission. Lilly would run screaming if she saw the effect she had on him. He exited the car and shut the door quietly before opening the back, offering his hand. Instead, Lilly pushed and shoved Annie at him so he held the miserable young woman by both arms as Lilly emerged, a vision in a day dress of turquoise with accents of green, her hair caught loosely on the nape of her neck. Simply dressed, but a lady with complicated opinions.

"I parked here to misdirect the neighbors but I'll walk you in," he said softly, alert to anyone up in the neighborhood, and Lilly nodded, her eyes speaking volumes he didn't dare interpret. Annie snivelled and tottered along between them.

Treading the stairs they entered the house. Mac noted the door wasn't locked and wondered at it. These people must live in a different world. The thought cooled his ardor. They *did* live in a different world, one he didn't fit into. However, he followed the two women inside, powerless against the flame that was Lilly.

"Thank you," she breathed, as she looped an arm around Annie whose drama appeared to be highly influenced by alcohol.

"I'll wait to make sure you don't need help," he asserted, and leaned against the closed door frame. "I'll wait right here."

Her lips parted and the tip of her tongue touched the upper one.

He contained himself with the practice of countless years.

The two figures made their way down the long hall and he couldn't tear his eyes away from the taller one. Her spine was straight, despite her burden and her curved hips swayed enticingly. He tortured himself just watching, oblivious to the style and decorations surrounding him. Then he waited, the settling sounds of the big house marked by the ticking of the mantel clock. He finally shifted to lean against the wall, away from the press of the large, brass doorknob.

At length she emerged from the back of the house, gliding down the hallway, the stuff of her dress flowing around long, slender thighs, her trim ankles flashing beneath the hem. He was amazed that her heels made such little sound on the highly polished floors. Was she a figment of his fevered imagination?

"She's asleep. It didn't take long, what with the emotional outburst and the several cups of alcohol. I refused to attend your speak with her earlier, but she got to drinking, and became so upset over Raymond, that …well, I couldn't let her go alone. " Lilly's voice was soft as velvet, even as her aspersion about the product he sold was very evident in the way her mouth pursed. Mac held his pose against the wall paneling with great difficulty, wanting to kiss those lips until they softened and parted for him.

"May we talk?" He had to start somewhere, and if he waited until the next day, the camaraderie forced by the need to get Annie home and safely into bed would be gone.

Lilly cast a look down the hall. "My aunt and uncle are abed, and they sleep heavily. But it would be the case tonight when my uncle would waken and seek refreshment and come upon us. I can't risk that."

"Then come to my house. You know it's not far. We won't be discovered or interrupted, and I'll show you back here before your relations arise in the morning."

As soon as the words left his mouth he knew he'd erred.

"Morning? You assume too much, Mr. Adair."

"I misspoke. I'll show you back as soon as our conversation concludes." He tried for a more placating tone but it was difficult to ease the roughness of his voice as he thought about having her alone in his quiet home.

That sweet pink lightly colored her cheeks and she looked anywhere but at him. "Perhaps tomorrow." He noticed she didn't deny they needed to talk, and the prickling tension was building rapidly between them again.

"Tonight, Lilly. After all, we should come up with a plan to defer the wagging tongues." He didn't have to explain further. She knew there would be many gossip fires to be put out tomorrow if at all possible. And he wasn't above the silver-tongued approach if it would get her somewhere in private with him. "We can't talk here. We might wake your aunt and uncle. Or the staff."

Lilly shook her head and clasped her hands behind her, causing the material across her breasts to tighten. Scooping her up and rushing her to his home without further ado was first and foremost in his mind. He quashed the idea, albeit with difficulty. But if she didn't stop looking so incredibly appealing he wasn't going to be responsible for his actions.

"For a short while then. And we'll use the side yard. I won't risk anyone noticing."

Once she caught up her light wrap and tiny purse, he offered her his arm and she slipped hers through to rest her little hand on his forearm. He fancied her touch burned right through his suit jacket but didn't imagine the crackling feel of their connection. The way she tensed and passed him a startled glance assured she felt it, too. Mac hustled her through the door, allowing it to close almost soundlessly behind them before guiding her down the steps and across the broad lawns separating their respective dwellings.

\*\*\*\*

Aside from a couple of minor stumbles, they gained his front steps in near silence, broken only by the faint sounds of night birds and flying insects. He wondered if Lilly could hear his heart beating out of his chest. So near and yet so far … he had no idea how he was going to present his suit when he got her inside his home, but surely the words would come to him.

Fumbling with the large key, he managed to open the mortise lock, shove the heavy door open, and flip on the hall light, all without losing his grip on Lilly. Then they were inside and he had no further excuse to touch her. Carefully extricating himself he thought to give her more space, becoming aware she hadn't stepped away, her face now turned up to his, eyes wide and lips parted. The illumination threw shadows in the depths of the hall, pooling at the base of the stairs. Mac didn't question anything—he took what was his, what had belonged to him since they'd met, and gave her himself.

Catching her to him, he crushed her against his chest and seized her mouth, his fantasy come true as she softened and parted for him. The kiss was both salvation and torment, her taste as memorable as before but spiced with greater need, and he accepted what she offered, giving back from the depths of his soul. She moaned, a sweet sound, and Mac dipped her slender frame, catching her up with one arm beneath her knees, the other supporting her back. He climbed the wide staircase from memory, lost in Lilly's flavor.

Shouldering through the door of his bedroom he paced to the big bed and lay her down on the satin counterpane, the rich burgundy and gold of the fabric a perfect foil for the turquoise and green of her dress. As their lips parted, he searched her eyes, looking for anything that might tell him she didn't want this. Nothing but glazed passion faced him and he straightened to pull his jacket off, careless with the expensive finery. She watched his every move as he yanked the shirt from his trousers, the cuff links pinging to the floor, the shirt itself joining the crumple of his jacket near the chair he'd tossed it toward. The light he'd left burning earlier lit the room sufficiently for him to surreptitiously palm a condom from the small container atop the dresser. He doubted he had the control to pull out once he gained purchase within her body.

Her eyes widened as he stepped fully into the light and he wondered what she saw. He was fit. He had to be to handle some of the issues behind the scenes at his joint, so his shoulders were packed with muscle, as were his arms. He'd always been broad in the chest from the manual labor foisted on him as he reached his teen years, in order to gain a crust. But did she see how his skin wasn't the pale, untried flesh of the men who moved in her circles? Did she see he was tan, and not from the sun?

Nothing but desire etched her fine features and his worry subsided. His own passion was too great to allow race to come between them. He dared hope she was as liberal as she protested to be. With a modicum of movement he unfastened and shoved his trousers down, biting back a curse when he realized he still wore his shoes. Awkwardly navigating to the chair with his ankles swathed in fabric wasn't the stuff of dreams, but he landed on the seat to yank off his shoes, leaving him in his silk underwear. He knew the thickness of his arousal would be outlined and obvious, but Lilly didn't flinch. She was a widow, so perhaps she wasn't easily discomfited by the male form. The little smile gracing her full mouth served to address any further thought. Maybe she'd found humor in his awkwardness, but it was also an invitation, one he accepted with alacrity.

Going to her, he sank down and gathered her close, kissing the curve of her throat as he began the laborious process of freeing the numerous buttons securing her dress at the back by feel. It seemed to take forever, but the taste of her skin and wondrous scent more than made up for it. At long last he was able to peel the material away until the dress pooled at her waist, baring the long line of her throat and shoulders above a slip of creamy lace. Was that him groaning? Her knowing look confirmed it and he knelt above her.

"You're beautiful, Lilly."

Smiling, she hitched away and he nearly tugged her back before her hands pushed at her dress until it passed her hips and slithered over her legs to slide to the floor. The clocked stockings held up by tiny pink garters were displayed beneath the slip, peeking out from under her step ins. Mac nearly spent himself at the sight and only by clenching his fists, crushing the satin of the bedding as he did so, was he able to bring his body under control. Was there a word better than beautiful? He suspected he needed to think of some.

Stroking a hand over her cheek, he leaned to feather another kiss on her mouth. "Beautiful."

"You cut a manly figure, Mac." Lilly's arms came up to enfold him and she kissed him back with enthusiasm as her body heated beneath his.

Passing his hands over every part of her he could reach while avoiding certain places, he reveled in her tiny sounds, stroking his tongue against hers as he explored the moist cavern of her mouth. She arched into him and held him tightly, his hard member throbbing for release against her soft belly, separated only by thin fabric. Unbidden, his hand gathered the silk of the slip and inched it up, the slip and slide of the material a sensual titillation. She gasped against his mouth and he freed her so they both could breathe.

"Sweetheart?"

"Mac, please…"

"Tell me what you want, Lilly. Anything."

"I want you. I can't think of anything else." Her eyes were dark, mysterious pools, glinting in the light. She pushed at the straps of her slip, and the breasts he'd been fixated on were unveiled, the round, plump mounds tipped with the pinkest buds. He groaned despite himself.

Diving in with more need than finesse he drew a nipple into his mouth, covering her other breast with a hand, cupping the tender weight filling his palm. Lilly whimpered under his touch and her hands moved restlessly, first on his shoulders, then drifting down his back to trace his buttocks. Mac doubted he could contain himself if she continued to touch him and grudgingly abandoned the taut peaks, kissing his way down her belly as he rolled the slip downward until he uncovered her step ins, the smooth cloth no deterrent for his determined hands. At last she lay clad only in her garters and stockings. Mac's heart stilled in his chest.

"God, Lilly. Look at you." He wanted to worship at her fount but didn't know where to begin. There was such depth to this woman, so modern, yet so earthy. She wanted this as much as he did, the scent of her arousal sharp on the air.

A tug at the waist of his undergarment put an end to his musings, the need to prolong and savor this unforeseen moment forgotten. He worked his last piece of clothing off and once again had to fight release as Lilly's soft hand gently caressed him. Lord help him.

"Loose me, woman, or this will be over before it fully starts."

"I'd say you've made a good *start*." The lilt of laughter in her throaty voice made him smile, too. He planned to finish as he'd begun.

Placing a hand at her apex he coaxed her thighs apart, the liquid heat of her pulling a growl of male satisfaction from his chest. He tested her readiness. Sliding a finger into her narrow sheath he marveled at how prepared she was for him. He pressed a kiss without warning right above his finger, the heady scent and taste of Lilly driving him on and his tongue flickered out to taste her.

"Mac!" Her thighs closed around him and she tensed.

"Shh, sweetheart. You're beautiful everywhere."

"But…" Lilly didn't appear to have experience with oral congress, something he'd be pleased to remedy in the near future. But he couldn't wait. He fumbled for the condom now reposing on the floor and covered up.

Making a place for himself between her legs was easy. She softened for him and gave him room to maneuver as he notched the head of his cock at her gate. Tight. Sweat beaded on his brow—he could feel it break free and trace its way over his temple as he fought for entry. She was so wet he slipped and slid in her copious juices, making her gasp as he stroked over the most sensitive part of her sex. A small hand grasped him to guide them into joining with a careful, lengthy push on his part.

Shuddering against her, waiting for her to adjust, he soaked in the awareness of being held, enclosed and enveloped in this woman. Had anything felt so good? Never.

"It's been so long," she breathed into his shoulder, the huff of her breath warm on his skin. "And it's different. So good."

He didn't want to think about any man possessing her before him. If he had his way he'd be the last and make it even better for her. He began to work above her, taking his weight up on his elbows as any gentleman should, not that he felt the least bit a gentleman. Rather, he wanted to unleash his beast, the animal craving its mate, and it took all his restraint to be gentle.

Lilly moved with him, the satin length of her outstripping the texture of the counterpane, bountiful breasts rubbing seductively against his own smooth chest, vying with the intensely pleasurable clasp of her around his shaft. It was a time of paradoxes, yet a time of certainty.

"More," she pleaded, thighs lifting against his hips and her hands gripping his upper arms. She arched into him and he gave over to the moment.

Her body writhed against the power of his thrusts, but she met him stroke for stroke until he felt his impending climax building. As his essence boiled forth he ground against her sex, and it was enough to take her with him to paradise. She called out his name, the abbreviation piercing his soul as she convulsed around him. He never wanted to leave the succor of her body.

Collapsing, tilting his weight to one side, he nuzzled into her shoulder, tasting the salt of her dewy skin, his tongue registering the slowing of her pulse as he slipped out of her body despite his need to stay.

"My Lilly."

They rested until the sheen of perspiration cooled and he rolled them to pull back the outer covers and tuck her beneath them, following to lie close. Her eyes were closed, the lashes feathering over her cheeks as tendrils of her hair curled around her forehead. He was struck again by her natural beauty—no artifice of heavy makeup and hair pomades for Lilly since that first night in his speak. He knew now she'd tried to fit in despite her principles, for her cousin.

Head turning, she gazed at him, her look soft and open, vulnerable. His chest actually hurt with the explosion of … love? Not just intense need, desire. She was everything. God.

"Mac?" What had his face told her? She wasn't meant for him. He wasn't worthy. He'd compromised her.

"Lilly, I don't have the words. Thank you, sweetheart." He didn't know how to tell her.

"I don't do this, Mac. I don't know... I mean, you must think—"

"Lilly. Never. You're a gift I don't deserve. Don't regret this." He gently tucked one of those tendrils behind her ear, wishing he dared to kiss her.

"Then what's wrong?"

He inched away, resolutely quashing the fantasy of waking up with her each and every day, hating what he was going to have to say, and unable to do so if their skin was still touching.

"I own a speakeasy, Lilly. I do things in order to keep it. I'm a criminal in many peoples' eyes. And I'm not part of your culture." He couldn't tell her she'd just made love with a half breed. It was his shame and secret to spare her.

Propping herself up on her elbow, her hand spearing through hair now flowing free from its restraint, she considered him. The sheet slipped to reveal the lovely swell of her breast and he longed to touch the creamy skin, holding hard against it. "Well, they do say opposites attract. I hadn't thought I'd meet someone like you and ... well, be with you like this, but I'm not sorry." The latter was said with Lilly's usual asperity around him and Mac fought a smile.

"I'm not sorry either, sweetheart, but I'm not for you. We can't do this, I fear." He feared a great deal, not the least of which was how society would view and treat Lilly, let alone individuals like the Knights should they discover his origins. No, it was better not to do this to her. How could he have been so stupid to give into his needs and seduce her?

Hurt flickered through her eyes and over her features. He ached to soothe her and somehow make this right.
\*\*\*\*

Lilly'd heard the term getting your wind knocked out, but she never thought she'd experience it with mere words being thrown her way. Surely it would have taken a physical blow to feel this hollow and agonized at the same time. Mac watched her as he leaned against the dark sheets of his bed, his straight black hair nearly obscuring eyes intent on hers.

"We already did do this." She made a desperate rebuttal as she took in his rejection, her pride beaten to the ground. He'd said she was a gift, but apparently she wasn't worthy of keeping any longer than it took to unwrap.

"I know, and it was wonderful, but we can't be together out there." He gestured at the wall, the door, maybe the ceiling for all she cared. "You know that."

Anger now heated her blood. She'd relented to her desires, accepted him into her body, and somehow she wasn't worthy to stand next to him on the sidewalk of Market Street? Gathering up the sheet against her bare body, Lilly struggled with herself. As soon as she'd agreed to walk to his house with him she'd known they would kiss again. As soon as they'd kissed, she'd known she would need to decide if she was going to let go of her ingrained morality or welcome a modern choice in her behavior. With Mac's hands on her and the ache he instilled in her, it had been an easy decision and one she'd fantasized about far too frequently to resist. She'd been curious and entranced and had fallen.

Rather than succumb to the tears of humiliation burning her eyes, she decided to attack with dark humor. "Really Mac, did you need to push me away so soon? It's not like I was angling for a ring. I'm a modern woman; I thoroughly understand men and women can engage in this sort of activity without any sort of commitment between them. Just as we did."

Scooting off the edge of the bed furthest from his long, powerful body, she sensed the tension her words had provoked in the man. She glanced away from his face to look for her undergarments on the cool, bare wood floor. The man needed a rug in here. At least she still had on her stockings. The bedcoverings made a shushing sound which was her only warning he'd risen. Before she could reach her step-ins crumpled against the wall, he'd grasped her arms and she raised her head up to find him frowning down at her, his swooping brows drawn into a knot on his broad forehead.

"What are you saying, Lilly?"

"I was perfectly clear. Perhaps your recent exertions have impacted your senses. Lie down until you feel better."

"Are you saying you're planning on doing this with someone else?"

"Aren't you? There were plenty of women on offer at your club. Women you'd feel more comfortable with."

"No." His low urgent tone echoed in some primitive portion of her brain and Lilly's intention to affect a cool response melted away. Tears pricked at her eyelids, no matter how much she fought them.

"You don't get to tell me no, not to anything." Breath waffling in and out with the pain of rejection, Lilly pulled against his grasp with a cry of frustration. At his touch, her body had flared to life again, warming and softening to him in primal betrayal. A modern woman might find herself flouting traditional roles, but she would never beg for attention from a man who'd rejected her. "Let me *go*."

Wordlessly, he raised his broad hands and took one step back. As Lilly collected her clothes she studiously avoided looking at the naked body he so casually displayed to her. She didn't need to look; the firm muscles, lean waist and hips, and tawny skin were indelibly illuminated in her mind's eye. So different than Daniel's pale, golden-fuzzed body. She'd called her late husband Danny-the-lion in jest, and as reference to the Bible tale, but there was no part of Mac's firm and burnished body that brought to mind scripture. Other than one of Lucifer's minions.

Wishing desperately for a folding screen to hide behind, she angled her body as well as she could to conceal herself from his unrelenting gaze as she donned her clothing. Slipping her dress over her head, she noticed torn fabric along the row of buttons and the memory of Mac's hands pulling at her made her weaken for a second. Enough. He'd made it clear he wished never to see her again and she was going to make sure to oblige him.

"Let me help—" He reached for her one more time and she flinched back.

"You can't go out with your dress hanging off. Turn around." His commanding growl didn't intimidate her, but his practical suggestion did mute her fury for a moment. Willing her muscles to remain still, she bent her head and tried not to notice his light touch dragging on the fabric as he drew the edges of her dress together and closed her up inside the soft cocoon.

Letting out a frustrated hiss of air as soon as she felt the last button slide into place, Lilly fled the bedroom, momentarily disoriented in the dark hallway. He'd carried her up and she'd been in such a state while in his arms she wasn't sure which way to turn. The dim glow of a light revealed the stairs and she walked quickly in that direction, the torn bits of her dress flapping between her shoulder blades. Taking the polished wooden stairs quickly, she slipped on several as she descended, barely catching herself as she sped up.

She was out the door and running across the lawn as the dew-drenched grass dampened her feet. She looked down, shocked to discover she'd left Mac's house without her shoes. Now the suppressed tears fell and she sobbed, pushing a hand against her mouth to deafen her hurt cries. Aunt and Uncle's window was open above to take in the cool night air her and she surely didn't want to waken them with such wretched sounds. Let that man keep her prettiest embossed leather shoes as souvenirs. She was never going back for them.

Stumbling up the wide stone front porch steps, she waited and sucked in a few deep breaths, hoping to calm herself enough to go silently through the hallways and hide in her room. She reached the door and twisted the heavy knob only to find it wouldn't turn. Who had locked the door?

Cold fear filled her, and Lilly's exhausted mind went blank for a moment. Was she going to have to sleep on one of the wicker sofas huddled on the porch? She certainly wasn't going to shuffle back to Mac Adair's house and seek shelter in his bordello-style bed. The back door was her last hope. She crept around the side of the house, doing her best to avoid sharp prickles of shrubbery in the dark, and climbed up the back porch, testing the doorknob. Exhaling with relief as it turned, she entered the dark kitchen and closed the door behind her with the softest possible click. The small wall sconce by the stove was on providing dim illumination and Lilly sighed with gratitude. She didn't relish the thought of jamming one of her unprotected toes against a chair or table leg and adding to the growing pain in her chest.

Just as she moved toward the door, a low voice growled out, "Look who we have here."

Breath stuttering in her chest as her heart seized, Lilly stared. Mrs. Kessler was seated at the table, swathed in a housecoat and staring at her with malice creasing her features, an unopened farmer's almanac on the table in front of her.

Somehow composing herself, she replied, "Good evening, Mrs. Kessler, I'm sorry to have disturbed you."

"Where have you been at this hour?" The older woman looked Lilly over. "Where are your shoes?"

With a sudden lurch, the weight of everything she'd been through that night fell on Lilly's shoulders and she slumped with exhaustion. Annie's idiotic and drunk adventure, her own unbelievable indiscretion with Mac, and now the censorious regard of the housekeeper. It was all too much to bear.

"It's no concern of yours." She didn't want the quaver in her voice but she was too tired to suppress it.

"Everything in this house is my concern, missy. Since you've arrived, the poor Beechly's have been at sixes and sevens. Don't think I haven't noticed your encouraging Miss Annie down the wrong path with your gallivanting about at all hours."

The unjustness of her accusations make Lilly shake. She didn't want to be disrespectful to the domestic, but the temptation to remonstrate the woman was strong. "I will repeat, Mrs. Kessler, my behavior is no concern of yours."

The housekeeper rose from her seat with a grunt, her face in shadow as she stared Lilly's way. "Don't think I don't know what immoralities you're getting up to. Going to your meetings unaccompanied, dragging Annie to that filthy speakeasy, and look at you now, arriving home in such a state."

The older woman stepped closer and Lilly forced herself to hold her ground and not back away into the

Hoosier cabinet behind her. Pale eyes stared into hers as Mrs. Kessler's face creased in a knowing smirk. "Hair mussed, dress creased, and look there, marks on your neck. Could you be any more indecent?"

"I tripped outside," Lilly managed to say as she edged toward the swinging door cutting her off from the rest of the house.

"More of your deceptions. You were with that new man next door, weren't you? He's just moved in and you're already over there fornicating. Comporting yourself like the Lilith you are. He's a bone-deep sinner same as you for all your pious airs. He goes in and out at all hours, up to no good."

Shaking her head once, Lilly pressed her hands against the smooth walnut of the door, unable to think of a proper response to such a terrible accusation. The idea that Mrs. Kessler knew who Mac was terrified her.

"Deny it all you like. Creatures like him get their comeuppance soon enough, good men see to that. And we all know what happens to hypocrites like you."

Lilly shook her head as she pushed at the door. She'd had enough. "Don't threaten me, Mrs. Kessler."

The housekeeper let out a dismissive snort and waved her hand like she was shooing a fly as she turned and walked toward the door to her room off the kitchen. Lilly turned and made her escape.

The heavy wooden panel swung shut behind her and she paused a moment in the dark back hallway, half expecting the woman to emerge and continue berating her. Such terrible comments and the anger behind them were distressing. Lilly resolved she'd have to bring up Mrs. Kessler's strange enmity with Aunt Eula and Uncle Wendell in the morning. If she could brazen through her own behavior.

As she quietly made her way up the stairs, muscles along the insides of her thighs twitched and the soft flesh between her legs ached, a painful reminder of the carnal acts she'd just indulged in with that man. It had been a long time since Danny, and as she reached her door and entered the safety of her bedroom, Lilly had to admit Mac Adair's dimensions and vigor had left their mark upon her. But all the physical evidence of what passed between them couldn't explain the ache in her heart.

## Chapter Seven

"Walter, I'm not interested in looking at curtains. Why ever would I be buying such things? Aunt and Uncle's are perfectly adequate and I don't have measurements to the farmhouse windows inscribed in my brain." Lilly tried to curb her impatience with him, but everything he'd said or done had irritated her beyond measure that afternoon. He'd called for her before noon and had accompanied her to luncheon, then insisted they take a stroll through the Gregg's department store downtown before bringing her back to the Beechly's.

She knew her annoyance was only partly due to Walter's intrinsic personality. Her soul was still smarting from Mac Adair's rejection, and truth be told, she was quite disappointed in herself. She'd behaved as recklessly as a flapper, with no thought to the consequences of her actions. It was a potent mix of bad feelings, and poor Walter was taking the brunt end of it.

The man in question smiled affably, her words seeming to have no effect and she wondered at his temperament. Mac Adair would sooner stop breathing than not respond to such a comment. Shaking her head and determined to banish thoughts of that cad to the dustbin where they belonged, she bestowed a smile on Walter and paid more attention to the gleaming glass and wood display cases surrounding them. They weren't in home furnishings as she'd suspected, but instead in the quiet and dignified jewelry department.

"We're not here to look at curtains, Lil." Walter gestured at a suit-clad salesman hovering nearby and the older gentleman strode over and inclined his head at them. Walter pressed one fingertip against the clear glass display top. "I'd like to see this tray in particular."

With a sinking feeling, Lilly focused on the black velvet covered square as the salesman removed it from the locked case and set it atop the counter. Diamond rings. Solitaires winking out all the colors of the rainbow. Oh no. How was it possible for her to have one man seeking to purchase an engagement ring when just a few hours before she'd been recklessly, delightedly, grasping another man's member to guide him into her body?

Shaking her head, she stared wordlessly at Walter as he grinned smugly back.

"She's overcome," he said as an aside to the placid man behind the counter, before bestowing his attention back on her. "They're impressive, I know. But considering my position, *our* future position in this city, you simply have to have the best. I won't have my wife overshadowed. What would that say about my business acumen?"

"These are the largest ones you have?" Walter turned to the salesman and he assured them these were indeed the largest diamond rings in Gregg's Department store.

Swallowing past the lump of distress lodged in her throat, Lilly looked down at the rings so she wouldn't have to stare at Walter's self-satisfied and clueless face. How could he have thought she'd want to be married to him? How could he have misread her character so wildly to assume she'd want such an ostentatious piece of jewelry? White gold bands glittered with swollen rose-cut stones and she drew in a breath, momentarily unsure how to decline such an unwanted gift and the obligation it represented.

"Try this one on, baby." Walter reached for her left hand and shoved on a cold ring even as she automatically drew back.

"No, Walter, I don't—"

"Not that one? Here, try this." He discarded the first and grabbed at another, all while keeping a tight hold on her wrist, almost as if he could sense her reluctance. Again he pushed it on her finger, heedless of her flinch or the resistance of her knuckle as he scraped the hard metal over her skin.

"Please stop." Lilly begged, glancing at the impassive sales clerk.

"Don't pretend modesty, my dear. This is the best choice for you. It's my duty as Daniel's cousin to care for his widow, manage the sale of your property and see you well set up to entertain my clients. It will be a perfectly successful future for us both."

There was an acquisitive gleam in Walter's eye she didn't like. She'd seen hints of it ever since she'd moved into town and he'd come calling under the guise of introducing her to the people who mattered.

"I don't wish to wear this," Lilly began, but Walter squeezed her wrist even tighter and leaned his head her way.

"It's done. Your aunt and uncle approve and we'll make the announcement as soon as you select a ring today. You've put me off long enough. There's no need for you to assume virginal hesitation."

Heat flooded her face and she shook. It was impossible for him to know what had transpired between her and Mac, but that primal encounter was never far from her thoughts. Hardly virginal indeed, in fact, she'd been quite wanton and had replayed their lovemaking many times over even though she should have stricken it from her mind.

The sales clerk cleared his throat, and embarrassment filled Lilly that he would overhear such private words. "Walter, no."

She pulled hard in an attempt to release her wrist and Walter jerked her closer, his eyes narrowing. Without warning, a broad tan hand clamped over Walter's, fingers pressing in between her skin and his.

Glancing behind her, she was somehow unsurprised to find Mac Adair glowering at Walter. Of course he would be there. Now her humiliation would be complete. "Release her immediately."

Walter's tea-colored eyes widened. "I know you, you're the owner of the speak. This is none of your concern, sir, and I'll overlook your bad manners if you unhand us immediately."

"What will you do if I don't?" Mac asked in a quiet growl as he bent the other man's fingers back. Lilly felt each one leave her skin with relief and as soon as she was free she clasped her twisted wrist close to her chest and took a step back from Walter. This placed her firmly against Mac's warm, solid body and her skin prickled. His free hand briefly touched her hip, then he nudged her to the side, all without removing his gaze or his grip from Walter. The other man sputtered as Mac advanced a step his way, bending Walter's captured arm at an awkward angle.

"Still waiting for you to do something. Walter, isn't it?"

Lilly stumbled as she edged away from the confrontation, only to find yet another man's hand on her arm. The thin fingers of the salesclerk beckoned for the ring still on her hand and she gladly wrenched it off and handed it over to him. Without pause he returned it to its place on the tray and set the collection back inside the case before locking it tight. Then he resumed his impassive observation of the few shoppers wandering the aisles, a slight curve on his lips. Goodness, this little episode would be the talk of the back room of Gregg's.

"I cannot believe you are assaulting me in such a manner," Walter babbled, his mouth open in shock as he retreated a step until he was firmly pressed against the jewelry counter, Mac looming over him with great concentration. Those bright blue eyes were narrowed and a slight smile played at the corner of his lips as he stared down at Walter.

"This is hardly assault. Let's go outside for that." Mac jerked his powerful arm once and Walter went sprawling along the wood floor between a case containing silver trays and another filled with cut crystal. He scrambled to his feet and turned to face Mac, red flushing his cheeks as he stumbled further away.

"Are you insane?"

"No, merely moody," Mac quipped and reached out to shove the other man into another case filled with tiny breakable things. Lilly gasped and reached for Mac's arm, a primitive part of her thrilling at the way she could feel his muscles flex under the thin wool of his jacket.

"Mac, please, no more."

He finally looked at her, his blue eyes dark with some masculine reaction she didn't want to understand. Her belly quivered and the pain of his rejection of her warred with a terrible and immediate urge to kiss him hard on his curved and mocking mouth.

He stared at her, his eyes locked with hers as silent seconds passed between them. Lilly struggled to control her breathing even as a tender ache built between her legs. He'd marked her as his and tossed her away. How dare he intervene now?

"As you wish." Mac looked away from her to favor Walter with a cool grin. "When a lady says no, she means no, Walter. Sorry to have to remind you so directly of that fact."

Smiling at the clerk behind the counter and tipping his hat at Lilly, Mac leaned down to gather up a large paper-wrapped package. He moved with relaxed ease past Walter who flinched and knocked himself against the display case again, upsetting a grouping of tiny glass animals. Lilly watched Mac's broad back as he exited the store and turned left, merging with the pedestrians visible through the wide plate glass windows. Despite his height and distinctive bearing, she soon lost sight of him in the crowd. Pushing away a strange sense of loss, she glanced at Walter. His shocked expression gave her hope that her imminent rejection of his suit might come as something of a relief to him.

"That ... that *savage*," Walter snarled. "Laying hands on an upstanding citizen such as myself." His hands trembled as they made an attempt to brush off his suit while he returned to her side.

Casting an eye at the salesman who now stood as if at attention, his gaze anywhere but on either of them, Walter continued to cast aspersions on Mac's character. "I'm surprised he didn't pull a blade and cut me. He has the look of someone of low breeding. That dark skin like a filthy immigrant."

Lilly'd had enough. Mac's skin was beautiful and so what if it was a contrast to paler hues? He could be Italian, Peruvian, or Mongolian for all she cared.

"I'll find my way home, Walter. And you needn't call again."

"Lilly!" He stepped toward her and gestured at the display cabinet. "Our engagement!"

"There is no *engagement*," she retorted, "except for the one you dreamed up in your head."

Throwing caution to the winds, she marched to the door and flung it open. She called over her shoulder,

disdaining even a look at Walter or the other interested bystanders, "Find yourself another nest egg, sir."
\*\*\*\*

Lilly adjusted her position on the narrow wood folding chair in the Methodist fellowship hall, the hard seat offering little comfort. She was still shaken by her encounter with Mac Adair at Gregg's Department Store, but strangely, whenever she recalled his quick and brutal actions towards erstwhile Walter, her only response was to flush warmly and sigh. She should be outraged but wasn't. Thinking on her dismissal of Walter afterwards didn't make her feel more than relieved to have it over. Maybe Mrs. Kessler was right. She was just a harlot pretending piety.

She was attending a lecture on the Children's League and couldn't wait for the speaker to finish so she could rise and stretch her legs and other tender parts. Her conversation with her aunt and uncle at noon about Mrs. Kessler had been futile. Whenever Lilly tried to explain their housekeeper's inexplicable antipathy, both older folks had tut-tutted and made the excuse that Mrs. Kessler was simply adjusting to having a new person in the household and that she'd soon settle. They asked for Lilly's patience and waved off her offer to return to the farm while declaring they loved having her in their home. They fortunately hadn't delved into her confrontation with the housekeeper, so perhaps the miserable woman hadn't spouted off her speculations. Not that Lilly wasn't prepared—she wasn't sharing any of what had transpired between her and Mac Adair and planned to deal with any aspersions on her character by not sinking to Mrs. Kessler's level.

Unwilling to press the issue and upset them, Lilly had made her way to the meeting and found the only available seat was between Peggy Finley and Vera

Longworth. Thankfully everyone in the audience had remained quiet during the lecture, but as the speaker stepped from the podium, Vera swiveled in her seat and quirked a sly smile.

"Lilly, I'm so sorry to hear about you and Walter. I can't claim to be surprised since your eccentric ways wouldn't have meshed well with his ambitions. I can just picture you lecturing folks to mind their speed when they'd drive off Walter's car lot. I imagine what you were up to the other night played a part in him breaking things off with you."

Cold dread seized her insides and Lilly commanded herself not to blush or stammer. Vera was like a cat, ready to pounce on any sign of weakness.

"What happened?" Peggy spoke up from the other side. "All *I* did was go through my stockings and re-roll them."

"I should say, we know what Annie did. Shameless, really. Your aunt and uncle must be mortified."

Letting out a sigh of relief, Lilly shook her head at Vera. "It wasn't all that dramatic. Annie and Raymond simply had a spat and we went home."

"Yes, but you got a ride home from that bootlegger. How'd you manage that?" Vera's knowing eyes held her own and Lilly's courage shriveled. If only this gossipy woman knew what else Lilly had managed, she'd slide onto the scuffed wood floor in shock. Or not.

"He offered."

"That's right, he lives next door to you so it was only natural." Peggy broke in with her innocent comment, blinking as both Lilly and Vera stared at her. "What? My brother's friend's father sold him the house. Glad to get it off the market, too."

"That's interesting," Vera purred. "So you have a neighborly connection with a notorious criminal."

"I wouldn't say we have a connection." Lilly struggled to forget the actual connection they'd forged. If she thought about how she'd groaned at the pleasure of their joining, reached her bliss so quickly, she'd flare with an embarrassment Vera couldn't possibly miss.

"Well, be that as it may, you might want to warn the salesman that house will be back on the market soon enough, Peggy."

"What are you talking about?" Lilly couldn't suppress the sharp tone in her voice as she turned back to Vera. A sharp foreboding filled her.

"Nothing really. Forget I said anything." The young woman played coy as she brushed her hands along her embroidered tan skirt and crossed her ankles.

Lilly wanted to grab Vera's pale plump arm and twist her skin until Vera cried out and revealed what she knew.

Peggy fluttered her hands. "Do you mean someone's going to take the house? He paid in cash, my brother said, so there shouldn't be any problems with a bank."

"Nothing like that. It's just that certain sections of Lima are due for a good cleaning, so to speak."

The Klan, she was talking about the Klan, Lilly realized with a cold shudder. Any personal dislike she might have for Mac evaporated at the thought of what horrible punishments might await him at the hands of those maniacs. She wouldn't find out any details from Vera if she acted as frightened as she now felt.

"A whitewashing?" Lilly was desperate to sound witty and unconcerned but bile filled her throat.

Vera laughed out loud. "Lilly, you are quick-witted. You always have been. My brothers were out this morning on an errand for the Knights. When Mr. Bonner at the hardware store heard why they were shopping, he even gave them a volume discount."

"But what did they buy?" Peggy asked, her eyes wide and wondering.

"Rope, kerosene, stakes. They're raiding Momma's laundry right now to get rags for torches."

Lilly's mouth was dry and her tongue felt like it had stuck to her teeth, but she managed to get the next question out. "When are they ... when will it happen?"

"Tonight, or if it rains, tomorrow. It's hard to get a good blaze going with damp wood." The woman tittered and waved at someone she knew on the other side of the hall. Lilly's stomach turned over. Mac, trapped in his burning speakeasy, his skin scorching, head thrown back in pain as the flames consumed him ... she couldn't get the hellish image out of her mind. Lilly stood up so abruptly her chair fell over with a loud clatter. Both Peggy and Vera drew back at her sudden move.

"I just remembered, I have to go pick up some pencils I ordered for the Sunday school classes. So nice seeing you." Lilly added the automatic courtesy as she stumbled away from the other women and walked toward the door, already calculating which trolley car would take her the closest to Mac's club.
****

Somehow a pebble had inserted itself into her shoe but Lilly kept walking, unwilling to take the time to shake it out when Mac was in danger. She'd chosen the wrong trolley and ended up having to walk several extra blocks, and her feet, ankles, and knees ached from covering so much pavement. Rain clouds were drawing close and she glanced at the darkening sky anxiously, hoping precipitation might deter the arsonists.

Turning a corner and stepping around a stack of abandoned and battered newspapers, she spotted the door to the speakeasy ahead. Rumbles of machinery and clangs of metal echoed from nearby factories. The street was deserted, with only a few parked cars and strewn trash to keep her company as she limped over to the entrance and rapped as hard as she could on the battered wood surface. Sweat trickled between her shoulder blades. She didn't remember the secret knock and only suspected someone would be there this time of day. Someone had to be about to accept shipments or clean before the crowds arrived later.

The door remained immobile and Lilly struck at it again, wincing at the pain in her hand as she hit it. Her fear and frustration simmered in her with sickening force. If no one opened it, she'd have to find the back alley and try again. Surely these industrial buildings had more than one entrance.

There was a muffled noise from inside and she sent out a fluttery breath. With rattles and squeals, the door swung open a few inches, chains still securing it top and bottom. A scowling face peered out at her. The man with the scarred face shook his head and quirked his lip in what likely passed for a smile. His eyes narrowed in recognition.

"No miss, not for another few hours. Go on home and eat your dinner, listen to the radio a bit before you come back."

"Sir, please, I'm not here for entertainment. I need—" The words caught in a sticky mess in her throat. She didn't want to say it but had no choice. "I need Mac Adair. I need to see him, rather."

"Bossman's in there. Come on then." His tired face disappeared along with the restraining chains after he looked her over front the toes of her scuffed shoes to the wisps of hair hanging from her loosened combs. The door swung wide. Yet again, Lilly had to enter this building under duress.

She knew her way and walked down the hallway, the pebble in her shoe still a torment as she hobbled into the main lounge area. Just tables with chairs stacked on them, the bar was abandoned. The only inhabitants were the band members, dressed casually in collarless shirts and full pants. The men on the dais stopped arranging their chairs and instrument cases when they spotted her.

"Help you, ma'am?" one of them spoke up after glancing at his peers.

"Mac Adair, if you could please direct me." She could barely get the words out, her mouth was so dry. Sucking in a breath, she waved her thanks to the men when several of them pointed to a set of stairs along the far wall she'd never noticed before.

Dreading the ascent, Lilly forced herself to walk over and take each step to her doom. The heels of her shoes thudded on the wood and echoed in the nearly empty space. With a sickening crack, one heel disconnected from the sole of her shoe and thumped down the stairs. Lilly watched it tumble but turned resolutely back to her climb. Holding onto the rail as a means to pull herself forward, Lilly made it to the top and took a glance around. A narrow walkway lined the far wall broken by a few illuminated windows. There were two doors, one open, the other closed.

With visions of flames consuming him, hot tar sizzling along his tawny skin, Lilly pushed herself to the open door and entered with an uneven lurch. There he was, seated behind a wooden desk, leaning back in a chair far enough that his polished shoes balanced along the top. As his head turned and he took in her presence, he swung to his feet with a hurried movement, the chair rolling into the wall with a hollow thud. A momentary flash of something in those pale eyes was quickly extinguished as an impassive mask settled over his features.

Her fluttering stomach clenched to a leaden mass and she almost folded over with the sensation. As much as her pride hurt, she had to warn him. It was what one civilized person owed another. Even if one of them was a heartless cad who'd inexplicably come to her aid with Annie.

"Lilly, what—" He moved from behind the desk and reached out a hand to her and she stepped away automatically, her balance uneven due to her mangled footwear, frightened of how his skin against hers might make her feel. *Say what you need to say and get out.*

"Mac, Mr. Adair." She swallowed again, desperate to pull her gaze away. He shuffled another step closer. She heard movement to her left and looked over to find another man in a pale shirt and dark trousers rising to his feet. She hadn't even noticed him.

Mac glanced over at the other man. "Mrs. Townsend, this is Phillip, my head bartender."

Automatic social courtesy steadied her and Lilly nodded a greeting and murmured a how-do-you-do. Phillip, after a glance at Mac, made his excuses and exited the room, softly closing the door behind him as he left. Now she was alone, trapped, with him and her heart clenched in her chest.

She shifted her feet, desperate to escape the regard of his probing gaze and the overwhelming presence of his body so near hers. The pebble in her shoe dug in and a wave of pain up her leg made her cry out and stumble against the door.

"Lilly, you look…" He narrowed his eyes as he took in her disordered appearance. "Sit down, over here."

Without waiting for her acquiescence, he grasped her elbow and towed her to a narrow davenport pushed up against one of the wood paneled walls. With a lurching limp, she found a seat, her legs trembling. He crouched in front of her and frowned, a tumble of blue-black hair obscuring his face.

"Your stockings and shoes are ruined. What were you doing? Why are you here?" His sharp comment and questions burst out as his hands grasped at her heel, levering off her shoe before she could reach down to discourage the familiarity. He raised her foot and the lack of pressure from the pernicious bit of rock made her sigh.

"Look at this, you're bleeding."

She was. Blood coated the bottom of her silk stocking in dark red, drying at the edges, bright and shiny where the obstruction had pressed into her flesh. Biting back a moan, she shook her head once. She'd simply force her footgear back on after she'd said what she needed.

"Mr. Adair—"

"Don't call me that," he hissed up at her, his eyes narrowed in anger even as his big hands cradled her injured foot. "Not when it's just you and me."

Working her dry lips together, she readjusted her approach. Simply convey her message and leave, that's all she had to do.

"Mac. I heard the Klan is coming for you. Maybe tonight, probably tomorrow."

He froze for a moment, his normally cool demeanor replaced by lines of worry. Within a breath, he was back to his usual implacable expression.

"They've been rumbling for a while." He shrugged his broad shoulders as he bent his head to inspect her foot. "Unroll this stocking."

"No!"

"It's ruined. I want to see your foot." His tone was so self-assured that anger burned away at the edges of her worry.

"I'm not taking off my clothes—"

"Just your stocking, woman." He looked up at her and frowned, something alight in his eyes as he challenged her.

Defiance wasn't going to get her anywhere but further embroiled with him, so she reached down, slid up the hem on her dress and bent her fingers around the garter's clasp. Her fingers shook and she struggled unsuccessfully with the metal ring and soft tab holding the knit silk.

Gusting out a hot breath she felt on the skin of her calf, Mac's fingertips intervened, easing apart the fastener with no trouble. She reminded herself he'd had plenty of practice with others as he rolled the tattered stocking down and gently pulled the soft material around her heel. The dried blood held the silk like adhesive and with a tearing sensation he removed it from her, dropping the ruined thing to the floor as he studied her foot.

"Torn up. What were you doing, marching around in a gravel pit protesting gin fizzes?"

Lilly gulped in a breath, too upset to respond. She'd rushed here heedlessly and he'd reacted to her warning like it didn't matter. All for naught, and here he was touching her body again and making her skin twitch like a horse bedeviled by a fly. The wound on her foot was awful looking; the rock had worn a large hole through her skin and it still oozed blood, and there were several blisters along her toes.

He supported her foot with one broad hand and as he shook his head and looked up at her, his other slid up to curve around the muscle of her calf. Mesmerized by the tiny caress and the heat in his eyes, Lilly fought a primitive urge to lie back on the sofa's cushions and encourage him to continue his inspection of her body.

"You can't go back looking like this. People will think you've been debauched. I'm taking you to a friend's. I'll get you home after I'm done." He rose and smoothed his cuffs.

"Done with what?" Lilly squeaked as he reached down and lifted her into his arms in a smooth motion. This brought her face close to his and she stared at him as she took in the pressure of his muscles arms around her back and under her knees.

"Done with those white-robed vigilantes."
\*\*\*\*

Rage wasn't an accurate description for the emotion eclipsing Mac's good sense, but the very blood in his veins boiled and flowed hotly in disregard of his efforts to marshal his thoughts. Lilly had *suffered* in her efforts to come and warn him of the machinations of that pack of cowardly individuals who dared called themselves the crusaders against moral turpitude. As if attacking the discriminated wasn't a hypocritical and immoral act.

He was certain many of their numbers populated his very speak each and every evening, if not the others in the state, and danced and clapped, immersed themselves in the music produced by the people they later disparaged. Hypocrites. He didn't give much thought to his own safety, but to think that Lilly had involved herself in this quagmire... His belly clenched at how the locals would treat her if they found out. It would be far worse than the marring of the silken skin of her foot.

At last he allowed himself to consider the deeper truth. Despite their sour parting after the most incredible intimacy he'd ever experienced, despite how he'd spoken to her and acted the brute with her companion, Walter,

Lilly had cared enough to flout tradition and risk her reputation to warn him. If he'd doubted her professed care and compassion, all her good deeds and intentions, he could hardly pretend any longer. And he also allowed himself the tiny spark of hope—that Lilly hadn't warned him purely because she believed it was the right and correct thing to do. Lilly had come to him because what they shared had meant as much to her as it did to him and she was damning the consequences. His rage faded before the hope and was replaced with such fear and anxiety he had to tighten his hold on her to still the shredding of his soul.

"You're crushing me," she protested faintly and he forced his muscles to release a tad.

"I don't want to drop you. These stairs are steep."

As she subsided against his chest, her head resting lightly on his shoulder and the fragrance she embodied wafting up around his face, he willed another reaction back as his shaft hardened with lust and adrenalin. This woman drew him like no other but there wasn't time for his need. He was going to take her to Maisie's and ask the other woman to shelter her for the time being. Maisie might look askance at a woman she'd see him favoring, but he knew all her secrets—alcohol tended to loosen people's tongues and pillow talk wasn't necessarily exclusive to men. The flirtatious flapper had a child she hid from public view.

Forced to sell her speak and take a low profile insofar as business went because of the risk to the little boy, Maisie held the KKK in utter contempt for the same reasons he did, even if they had different motivations.

"Where are we going?" Was it his imagination or was Lilly's tone somewhat languid, to match her body's trusting stance in his arms?

"I have a … friend I'll take you to. On the other side of town. I'll drop you there, then return and take care of business."

Obviously it was the wrong thing to say. She tensed and craned her neck to stare into his face, her tousled locks drifting over his upper arm. He wished there was no material between them. "I don't think that's a good idea."

"What? You going to my friend's? Or me dealing with the KKK?"

"Who is this friend?" He carefully set her on her feet beside his car, Dennis having opened the door for them after checking the alley with great care. The man never seemed to sleep. Without answering he opened the passenger side and coaxed her inside, taking pains not to brush his hand down her cheek. If he touched her again in an intimate manner he'd drive off with her and never look back. Maybe he should do that anyhow. Instead, he contented himself with checking her abused feet and dusting off the slight detritus from her brief stance by the car.

"Someone I've known for a long time. She has no love for the Knights and will stand by me. Us." He dared hope there was an "us" because he was reconsidering his chivalrous thoughts of not being good enough for her. He wasn't, but he couldn't stand the thought of denying himself. And not spending the next forty years proving himself.

Lilly stared into his eyes, and he let her in past all the shields he'd built over the years, in to read the true Mac Adair. As she reached for his hand, fresh color tinted her cheeks and he breathed a sigh of relief to see her pallor improve. He gently tugged his hand free, after experiencing a bout of reassurance, then shut the door and hustled around the hood to climb into the driver's seat, his heart soaring despite their predicament. He had to focus on dealing with the Knights for now, but Lilly still deserved to know the whole truth before she bound herself even closer to him.

Over the roar of the motor and the squeak and bounce of the tires and suspension, he gathered all his courage and spoke again. "They're very dangerous. You need to know that my business isn't the only reason they would target me, if anyone knew the truth."

The seconds stretched painfully. He was aware of Lilly waiting quietly at his side.

"I'm part Shawnee, through my mother." There, he'd said the plain truth and could only wait for her reaction. If she rejected him, he'd be grateful she would be removed from his life and the dangers that might come his way. He hardly dared dream she'd respond with acceptance. Tearing his gaze away from the windshield, blurred by the increasingly heavy rain, he risked a look at her.

"It doesn't matter to me. At all. And I think I already knew." Her assertion fell between them and he somehow managed to pick up the first part.

"How could it not matter, Lilly?" He looked again in her direction and met her gaze, full of compassion and—love?

"Because I'm a modern woman, Mac Adair," she replied with a touch of her usual asperity. "But mostly because…because I…feel something for you. I know how I felt about you before, and my impression of you remains unaltered now that I know. On that you can rely."

Mac's head pounded with such disbelief, even as his chest swelled with deep emotion. Ah, that was his Lilly, all spirit and heat and incredible loyalty. "I feel *something* for you, too, Lilly. A considerable something.

And I plan to explore that something with you as soon as this mess is dealt with. Explore it with you in my bed as well."

"You'll have to speak sweeter to me than that, sir." The quiver in Lilly's voice and the way the register in her tone dropped convinced him she was thinking along the same lines so he contented himself with a smile. He caught a similar lift of her sweet lips from the corner of his eye and he chastised his body's one track mind to make good on his promise immediately.

"How did you know?" he then asked quietly. "About my heritage?"

"Your skin is tan, despite working inside. Tan all over." He knew a charming blush would be tinting Lilly's fair skin.

"Your pale blue eyes distract a person, but your hair is so black, like a crow's wing. And your profile reminds me of those pictures in the almanacs. Of proud Indian scouts."

"My father was white, my mother maybe half," he offered, surprised that his usual bitter feelings whenever he mentioned the man who sired him were less painful. "He rarely came to visit us, my mother and I."

"Shame on him," she muttered and Mac's belly clenched at the anger and protectiveness in her tone.

"He's dead. No worries."

She was silent but he could feel her outrage. Not pity or sanction, but impatience and anger with the man who helped create him, then apparently found him an embarrassment. The memory of a tall, blond, blue-eyed giant who awkwardly patted him on the head and slipped him a coin swirled through his memory. Mac flinched and tightened his grip on the wheel even further. Where had *that* come from?

Maybe he had to let go of all the bitterness and remember the bias of the time. Maybe his father would have done better by them had he not been taken so precipitously. Lilly's small hand crept over to rest on his bicep. He soaked in the comfort and fiercely told himself he'd be there for his own child no matter what, and found himself actually contemplating the idea of being a parent. He wanted Lilly so fiercely his teeth ached, as his lover, his confidante, his wife. And maybe, someday, the mother of his children.

"We have so much to talk about, Mac," Lilly suggested, and slid her hand from his arm to place it gently on his thigh.

"That we do."

The rest of the drive passed in silence of the comfortable kind, if heady with sweet desire. No matter the risk he must inevitably confront, Mac mused on the irrepressible needs of people in love. Head over heels. Love at first sight. Incredible but true, just like the ideas presented in those infernal reading and writing classes his aunt had insisted he attend in Lima, hiding his Shawnee roots. He wondered where Lilly had learned about romance and love and hoped she'd share with him. He envied her husband his time with her.

Pulling up to Maisie's with a jerk and a sputter, Mac turned to observe Lilly considering the attractive cottage with interest. The place was set back from the road within a veritable grove of mature white oaks and Canadian yew. The great trees nearly overshadowed the nicely manicured yard and flower beds. Not for the first time, Mac wondered at the dichotomy that was Maisie. But then, living in this side of town, away from prying eyes was probably the most suitable. He cranked the door open and made his way around to help Lilly out.

"I can walk."

"Not without your shoes, sweetheart." He tasted the endearment, the first he'd expressed to a woman outside of bed-sport, and it tasted fine. From her startled, then pleased look, she thought so, too.

Swinging her up, he strode up the winding path to the front door, the deeply set windows resembling offset eyes. Before he could ask Lilly to raise the knocker, the door swung open and Maisie's astonished face filled his vision.

"Mac!" She raised her eyebrows then narrowed her eyes on Lilly who gave a little hitch against his chest.

"Maisie. This is Lilly." He decided not to share last names at that moment. "She needs help."

Lilly muttered something he didn't catch, but Maisie's eyes widened and she smiled slightly. "Come in, then."

He followed the other woman inside, his precious burden now making movements and sounds that signaled her desire to be set down and he reluctantly obliged her. She was so slight and tiny beside him and his protective instinct surged again. Maisie directed them into a large room just off the entry hall and asked them to sit.

Mac decided to speak plainly. "The Knights have my speak in their sights. The speak and the orchestra. Lilly overheard some plan and came to warn me."

"I see." Maisie looked between them, her glance encompassing Lilly's disheveled appearance, but no judgment clouded her pretty features.

"Ma'am?" A little voice spoke from the archway and all the adults turned to face the child. The small boy was slightly darker skinned than Mac. His hair was a medium brown, falling in loose curls around his head and his eyes—topaz perhaps, or citrine.

"This is Arthur." Nothing in Maisie's tone was open to interpretation.

Lilly smiled at the boy, a warm, caring expression the child spontaneously returned, the initial wariness on his handsome features melting like spring snow in the face of direct sunlight. He edged into room and went straight to Maisie who held out her hand to him. He clambered up into her lap. Mac watched as Lilly worked out the child's parentage and noted her total lack of disdain or contempt. As did Maisie.

"So you'd like…Lilly…to stay here for a short while?" Without her heavy makeup, her golden hair now loose and flowing around the shoulders of her housedress, Maisie looked an innocent, a far cry from the jezebel of his speak. Even her speech, both the cadence and grammatical structures, was vastly different. A perfect disguise, he supposed, much like his own. Mac experienced a moment of regret that he had taken her at such face value when they'd first met.

"I—"

"I'm—"

They both spoke at once, eliciting an amused glance from Maisie. "Perhaps Lilly might speak for herself, Mac, darling."

He didn't particularly care for the way Lilly looked first at him and then Maisie, but she spoke calmly and politely. "Mac is concerned for me. And my reputation, no doubt. I personally don't care."

Before he could remonstrate, Maisie spoke. "It'll be more than your reputation, Lilly, if the Knights see you as even remotely involved with the owner of a speak or championing those they see as inferior. Your reputation might be in tatters, but your person may well never recover."

Lilly sat taller, and tilted her head. Mac braced for a tirade. "I see. Well then, I suppose I must defer to people who understand best how to deal with such animals. You'll have to teach me what I can do to make a difference, because we can't let them get away with this! Knowing how to arrange the place cards at a supper isn't much use in this situation, but I have to do something."

"I'll deal with it, Lilly," Mac said. "I'm not without resources and thanks to you, I'm forewarned. But if you aren't safe I'll be distracted, and then something might happen the way you fear."

"I'm a woman of action," she protested. "Surely there's something I can do."

"Why don't we let Mac head back and put his 'resources' into place," Maisie suggested. "We'll have tea and you can tell me how you came to find out about the Knight's nefarious plans. And what happened to your poor foot. Where *are* your shoes?"

"Can we come up with our own battle plan?"

Mac gritted his teeth and let Maisie continue the conversation. When he got Lilly alone in his bed he was going to explain to her the appropriate roles of men and women with thoroughness.

But Maisie's eyes glinted with mischief. "We certainly can. Now, let me call Hester to get you a basin for your feet. Arthur will probably enjoy some cakes with tea. Won't you, my love? Can you fetch Hester?"

The hitherto silent boy nodded, his amazing eyes shining. He scrambled from his mother's lap, crowing, "Cakes. Cakes." They all watched with smiles as he raced from the room, presumably to look for Hester. Maisie rose to her feet and followed in his wake, studiously avoiding Mac's eyes.

In the ensuing quiet, Lilly inched sideways until her thigh brushed his and Mac held hard against taking her in his arms and kissing her senseless. He doubted it would totally distract her from any *battle plan,* but he would still like to try. She feathered her fingers down his forearm and he lost his own battle, reaching to drag her onto his lap, crushing her tightly against him to take her mouth with his own.

Her soft lips parted against his insistent tongue and he explored the sweetness of her mouth until the lack of oxygen forced them apart. Lilly sagged against him, eyes drooping with the intensity of their passion. Her soft buttocks caressed his aching cock and with great restraint he didn't rock her upon him.

"I need to know you'll be far away from the action, Lilly. Please."

"I'm not used to avoiding—"

"I know that already, sweetheart. Despite our short acquaintance. I know you don't run from a challenge or trouble. But this is ... far more dangerous than you realize."

With a sigh, she pressed her lips to his cheek, then kissed down over his jaw to his neck, her hands drifting around his shoulders. Mac closed his eyes and prayed tonight would work out. He wasn't going to leave this woman again, after today, nor ask her to leave him without the belief they had a future. He'd settle the issue without further ado.

A heavyset woman marched into the room, carrying a steaming bowl of water she carefully set on the small stool tucked close to the couch. Lilly slipped from her perch and adjusted her clothing with quick, nervous movements. If she was embarrassed by their proximity that was the only way she indicated it. Arthur ran in bearing towels and a roll of bandage, his face alight with the adventure.

"Miss Maisie is arranging tea. I'm Hester. She said for you to take care of your foot?" The woman peered at Lilly, her brow creasing in concern. "I see you've an injury. Do you need help?"

"No thank you, Hester. I'm Lilly. And this is Mac. I'll take care of my foot."

"I'll send Arthur back with some ointment, then."

Hester hove out of view, little Arthur dancing in her wake, and Mac snatched Lilly up to carry her over and seat her in front of the water bowl. A small sliver of soap floated on the top. Before she could reject his aid, he carefully raised her leg and lowered her injured foot into the water, wincing along with her at the obvious sting until she relaxed.

"That feels good, now the initial smart is over. No, Mac. You don't have to do that."

Ignoring her, he lathered the orange soap into a bubbly white and cleansed her foot, noting that the bleeding had nearly stopped, then rinsed the suds off and lifted it out to wrap it in a towel. "Put your other foot in, Lilly. You'll match that way."

Humor coloring her tone, she did as he asked, maybe for the first and last time. "There. Happy?"

He didn't answer, but let his fingers do the talking, quickly washing her other foot before moving them up the silk and curve of her calf to trace her inner thigh.

"Mac!"

"*Now* I'm happy." He moved the water and utilized the other towel. Lilly's feet looked huge and awkward in their shrouds, so different from the elegant, narrow length he knew them to be. He suppressed a smile and kept his mouth shut. "I'll bandage the cut as soon as Arthur returns."

As if his words conjured the boy, Arthur rushed in and presented a small tube. Mac took it with the appropriate appreciation and the child hunkered down to watch the doctoring. The small injury looked much better and Lilly hardly flinched when he applied the ointment, followed by the bandage. Mac had never felt better, taking care of this woman, and smiled up at her from where he knelt. He read her acknowledgement of the symbolism in her eyes and if Arthur hadn't been present he'd have kissed her again.

Hester interrupted their tender regard, lugging a huge tray of tea and dainties, and Arthur hustled to ensure the coffee table was clear. He stared with awe at the spread and put both hands behind his back, presumably to manage his temptation. Mac was uncomfortably reminded of his first visit to his aunt's, the victuals offered far too much for a child who'd never seen the like. He suspected that Arthur, who was obviously well cared for, was enamored with sweets and was observing a largess reserved for company. He doubted Maisie had many people taking part in this kind of hospitality, given her isolation.

Maisie glided in with a new grey silk dress on, a hint of the flapper in her movements, and he thought she'd probably regrouped, unwilling to show any more vulnerability in his presence. Didn't she realize he'd put himself at her mercy with entrusting Lilly to her care? Perhaps she did, because she crossed to sit beside Lilly and he straightened to his feet, one knee popping audibly. He refused to acknowledge it, an old injury before he learned to use his brains instead of his brawn.

"I won't tarry. I'll return as soon as possible." He found he didn't want to leave, but he couldn't stay either. Lilly regarded him, clearly trying to veil her worry and concern. He was struck by a thought.

"Where do your relatives think you are?"

She blinked and slowly shook her head. "They know I went to the lecture at the church and will assume I met up with friends. But perhaps I should send a note, the telephone isn't reliable."

"I don't have one as yet," Maisie spoke up.

"Then quickly pen one, Lilly. I'll see it gets delivered." He took a breath. "Tell them you'll be back in the morning."

Hester had long since removed herself from the room, and Arthur was still entranced with the food, but Maisie heard the inference loud and clear. Wherever Lilly was going to be tonight, it would be with him. However, Maisie busied herself with plates and saucers, pouring tea and admonishing Arthur to mind his manners, while Lilly wrote a note on some paper she retrieved from her small satchel, her cheeks high with color. But she didn't say anything in response to his innuendo, reminding him of her classy forbearance when in the company of others. He ruefully thought he might learn a thing or two.

He folded the scrap of paper, tucking it into his watch pocket, aware she followed his movements, her body leaning slightly toward him. Throwing class to the winds he pressed a kiss on her temple before making an awkward bow to her and Maisie, hampered by his semi-tumescence. Aware he was leaving Lilly to have any sort of frank conversation with a woman he'd also known in a biblical sense made him wonder if challenging the KKK wasn't perhaps the less dangerous part of the night he had yet to face.

"You take care, Mac. Lilly will be fine." Maisie looked as though butter wouldn't melt and he accepted his fate, heading out the door.

## Chapter Eight

Lilly glanced around Maisie's parlor to distract herself from how the skin on her temple still tingled from Mac's brief caress. She didn't care to analyze her behavior or reactions very closely, since everything around her was shifting in directions she didn't understand.

Her hostess's home appeared modest and well cared for from the exterior, but inside was a different story. Fine carpets, heavy silk draperies, and down-stuffed cushions on the fashionable furniture painted the picture of a woman who presented a different face to the world than the one she held in private. Lilly tried not to feel uncomfortable with bare feet and rumpled clothing as she accepted a cup of fragrant tea in a fine porcelain cup.

The little boy, Arthur, watched her with bright and intelligent eyes whenever he wasn't taking inventory of the pastries on the tiered tray. She smiled at him and he grinned back before his mother warned him he could select one, and one only, cookie. His little hand shot out and snagged the largest dessert, and Lilly tried not to laugh at his practicality. Rain pattered on the roof overhead and she could almost fool herself into believing this was merely a pleasant social call instead of a desperate moment dictated by the threat of vigilantes. Once again she was grateful for the rainfall.

"Sweetheart, use a plate and sit still on the chair when you eat that. I don't want to see a crumb or hear a peep. Miss Lilly and I need to talk," the blonde woman warned her son and turned her knowing blue eyes on Lilly as she sipped her own cup of tea. Mac had introduced her as Maisie, and Lilly hoped her emotional confusion regarding the man wasn't coloring her impressions of her hostess. It was clear Mac and Maisie knew each other well. Something had passed unspoken between the two when Mac had announced his intentions, but Lilly wasn't sure what it meant.

"Thank you for your hospitality." Lilly's manners won out over her suspicion.

"Anything for Mac." Maisie replied as she twisted the handle of the creamer towards Lilly. "Pardon me, I forgot to ask if you take milk."

"No, thank you. I prefer it plain."

One of Maisie's fine eyebrows arched up. "So, now that the pleasantries are concluded, perhaps you can answer a few questions, especially as it concerns the Klan. I have a rather … personal interest in monitoring their intentions and activities."

Lilly didn't look over at Arthur as he munched on his cookie with single-minded devotion. There was no need to draw attention to the little boy and the unfair position society had put him in. Like he had a choice in what his parents had done. "To put it plainly—"

"You seem to favor plain." The other woman shot back with a brief glance at Lilly's unadorned linen shift, now crumpled and dusty. Her hostess had changed into a heavily embroidered grey silk dress in keeping with her elegant surroundings. Lilly straightened her back. The other woman was lushly beautiful and exquisitely dressed, appealing enough to turn any man's head. Including Mac's. A small shiver of jealousy heated her blood, but she ignored it. If Maisie and Mac had known each other in an intimate way, it was none of her business at the moment.

"I do. In all things. In answer to your question, I was speaking with an acquaintance at the conclusion of a lecture today and she mentioned the imminent attack on Mac's club. Apparently he and his activities have been of interest to that organization of fools for some time."

"Who?"

Lilly wasn't sure to whom she was referring and her confusion must have shown.

"Who was your friend that spilled the beans?"

"Oh. It was Vera Longworth. Do you know her?"

"Know of her. Know her brothers a bit better." Maisie narrowed her eyes and Lilly's curiosity grew. What sort of woman had Mac left her with while he went out and faced danger on his own?

"Their sort is easily handled. It's the fellas in charge I worry about."

"I agree absolutely. I simply cannot sit here while such terrible things might be taking place." Lilly wished passionately for her shoes so she could leave and look for a conveyance of some sort. Where she'd go once she'd found one, she wasn't sure, but at least she'd be on the move and not parked to the side like a useless appendage.

"Not much you could do if you were in the thick of it." Maisie gestured at Lilly's injured feet.

"Perhaps I might borrow a pair of shoes."

"Not the right size." Maisie extended a silken-clad leg and showed off a dainty emerald satin pump cradling a foot at least two inches shorter than Lilly's own.

"Perhaps Hester—"

Maisie shook her head definitively and returned her teacup to its saucer. Arthur glanced at his mother and rolled off the sofa to retrieve a metal truck from under a nearby table. "Not a match either. Besides, Mac said for you to stay until he returns and stay you shall."

"Whatever for? I hardly owe him obedience." Her rebuttal was automatic, but something stirred in her even as she denied it. She didn't want to obey Mac, but she did want to … please him. Just as she wanted him to please her. Even as this realization dawned, Lilly felt a betraying blush heat up her cheeks.

"Call it what you will. I respect the man more than I do most of them, but he's not wrong to want you away from his property while he makes his arrangements. Not that it'll do him much good."

The other woman's dire tone made Lilly forget her momentary lapse into consideration of how much she wanted Mac's hands pleasing her. "Then you understand he's in terrible danger. I can't just sit here and wait to hear he's been, that he's—"

She broke off with a gulp, fear for him closing her throat in a painful obstruction.

Maisie gave her a sharp glance. "I'm not saying we do nothing, Lilly. I'm saying we do something more effective than hauling kegs of liquor and checking our guns every minute."

Guns? Mac was armed? The thought was both a comfort and terrifying. But Maisie and Mac were more experienced in this world, so it would behoove her to listen.

"What can I, what can *we* do, then?"

"Other than pray this rain falls harder tonight, I'd say we use what the Lord gave us."

Confused again, Lilly merely shook her head. The past few hours had been so entirely outside her normal experience she was completely disoriented at this point.

"Just because we don't have burly arms and bluster doesn't mean we're weak. We have the honey to distract those buzzing bees right away from whatever's gotten them swarmed up and ready to sting." Maisie leaned back slightly in her seat and gave a sly grin. "Arthur, sweetheart, you go see how Hester's getting along with dinner and ask her to come in here directly. Ask her for a plate, though I doubt you'll eat considering you just gobbled down that cookie."

Little Arthur rushed from the room on skinny legs, after giving Lilly another smile. How she would have loved to have had a child such as that. If she and Daniel had succeeded, her own might have been about that age. Could Mac be the little boy's ... no, their coloring wasn't similar enough. Now considering the idea of Mac's child, she could almost see a serious little boy with black hair and a straight back staring at her, or a laughing little girl with sparkling blue eyes curling in her lap for a hug.

"Do you have a child?" Maisie's unexpected question distracted Lilly from her melancholy thoughts.

"No, I wasn't blessed in my marriage."

"Married?"

"Widowed, nearly four years now."

"The war?"

"No, he survived that and the influenza, too. He was turning the crank on a Fordson tractor at a fair demonstration and something flew off and hit him on the head." Maisie's indrawn breath gave Lilly pause, but she soon continued. "He lingered for eight days, but then passed on."

Those were dark and bleak days and Lilly closed her eyes once, remembering how helpless she'd felt then. Her poor Daniel, broken in their bed as she'd crouched at his side, the life leaching from him with every labored breath he took. The frustration she'd experienced then was akin to her inability to make any sort of contribution now. "You were saying something about honey?"

"I was. Once Hester...ah, there she is," Maisie said and turned to smile at her returning housekeeper. "I'd like you to send your fellow off with some notes to deliver, if you please. I know it's raining and I wouldn't ask if it wasn't terribly important."

The other woman nodded and glanced at Lilly.

"I believe our guest will be staying for dinner so please set a place for her." Maisie sent Hester off with another dazzling smile. Once the housekeeper had disappeared down the hallway towards the back of the house, Maisie rose and went to a small rosewood desk where she pulled some note cards from a drawer. After selecting a pen, she wrote, leaving Lilly to feel even more useless as the rain pattered on the roof overhead.

"I'm just going to make a few suggestions to some ladies of my acquaintance. Mac would call it something crude like calling in favors, but I don't operate with such a heavy hand."

Maisie scrawled a few more lines on envelopes and rapidly stacked the notes as there was a shuffling sound from the hallway. "Ah, there you are Polk, perfectly on time as usual."

Lilly looked up to find a tall, imposing man in a slicker standing a few feet away. He gave her a glance from dark eyes and accepted the notes from Maisie with a nod. He turned and left the room nearly as silently as he'd arrived.

"As I was saying, a woman can wage war as effectively as any man. It's just wiser to employ less obvious tactics. Have you read about Lysistrata? I believe we should employ her technique with a slightly different spin. We're emancipated women after all."

Lilly blinked, overwhelmed by reference to the ancient Greek play from this enigmatic woman. "I'm not grasping your point."

Maisie chuckled, a deep, confident sound that made Lilly smile despite herself. "It's not my point which will be grasped. My friends have, shall we say, involvements, with several men in roles of leadership, both officially elected and within our less than savory Klan. I merely asked that they make the necessary overtures and exert themselves to, ah, distract these fellows tonight and as well as they can into tomorrow. Merely to give Mac a little breathing space. Between this soaking rain and the lure of honeypots, I doubt the Knights will be burning anything tonight."

A satisfied smile smirked over Maisie's mouth and Lilly was amazed at her cunning.

"But that leaves us with you." Her hostess rose from her seat at the desk and came to sit beside Lilly. She looked over the bandage and nodded once. "I hope I can rely on you to provide equal distraction to Mac once he returns. If he's safely out of sight for a time, all the better, hmm?"

At this provocative announcement, a rumble of thunder echoed and there was a loud rapping on the door. Both Lilly and Maisie jumped and stared at the entry.
\*\*\*\*

Mac stared impatiently at the painted wooden door. He was wet and discomfited, uncomfortable, and while the wooden panels stood between him and Lilly, a worm of unease wiggled in the back of his mind. Like any other male in a similar situation he hadn't been able to dismiss the worry that Lilly and Maisie had been discussing him—possibly coming to the conclusion they both knew him. In a carnal way. Didn't women gossip and ferret all sorts of information out? And they'd had a few hours together to chat. What had he been thinking?

But it wasn't like he'd had any other choice. Lilly had to be tucked away somewhere safe until he could deal with the Knights. As it was, things felt faintly anticlimactic. His biggest worry was the response from that housekeeper. The woman had looked positively evil when he stopped at Lilly's relatives' home to relay her message. Like she'd seen clear into his soul and wanted to gut him.

Hester filled the doorway, her wide face with its heavy features a match for her body. He'd been so lost in thought he hadn't heard her open it. He forced a smile and she nodded back, reaching to take his drenched hat, the brim bowing beneath the weight of the drizzle it had soaked up.

"Better give me your coat too, sir. I'll set it to dry. Unless you're off again quick."

"I expect I'll be here awhile, Hester, thanks." *Unless your mistress and my... my Lilly have formed a united front and want my guts for garters, having discussed my involvement with both of them.*

"Fine, sir. Miss Maisie has invited Miss Lilly for our evening meal." Ah, the women had indeed united. He hadn't thought Lilly could have gone far without her shoes, but she had a temper and he fancied she was a tad possessive. He *wanted* to feel her possession. His lower body stirred at the thought.

Steeling himself, he made his way into the living area. Arthur's little face gazed up at him from his sprawl on the floor, busy little hands hiding the evidence of crumbs at the edge of the carpet. Despite himself, Mac lowered a lid in the child's direction, men united. Then he chanced at look at the women. Lilly still looked charmingly disheveled, her cheeks flushed and beautiful eyes bright as they rested on him.

Dragging his fascinated gaze from her, he looked at Maisie. Once again, it was difficult to reconcile the poised, sophisticated "at home" woman with the flapper who frequented his speak. She favored him with a cool smile.

"Back so soon?"

Shrugging, he didn't wait to be asked. He chose the chair closest to Lilly, her scent just noticeable and he inhaled surreptitiously, pretending not to notice Maisie's speculative stare. He'd have preferred to sit beside Lilly, but placing himself between the two women seemed the height of stupidity. Lilly leaned forward slightly, closing the distance between them.

"I was able to connect with my—well, suffice it to say, the police presence in the area of my speak won't be lacking tonight." Finnegan had had his hand out a mile, but Mac wasn't about to quibble about money. The cop wasn't stupid. He knew that if Mac's speak was closed down, even temporarily, his lucrative side business of collecting bribes and protection money, would suffer a considerable blow to his wallet. Regardless, it bought him some time.

"That's tonight taken care of," Lilly said practically, not even reacting to his reference about blatant corruption in the police force. Mac felt such a pinch of guilt that he knew it'd tracked across his face. What was he thinking? She shouldn't be exposed to the seamier side of life. A flicker of thought, an idea, surfaced in his brain and he marked it for another time.

"Tonight," he agreed. "But it'll buy us … me at little time to come up with a plan."

A remarkably similar smile curved both women's mouths. The fullness of Lilly's rose-colored lips held the bulk of his attention, but Maisie's wide mouth mirrored hers in the moment. He sat up and fixed them both with his trademark glare, the one that had his staff putting their backs into their work and those hiding secrets confessing with alacrity.

"What have you done?" he asked quietly.

"I haven't done much of anything, Mac, aside from sit in awe of Maisie's skill and connections."

Maisie preened a little and the stuff of her dress rustled in the sudden silence. She raised one shoulder in a seductive manner. There was the flapper, and Lilly narrowed her eyes—on him. His belly tightened and he immediately strove to distract her.

"Maisie, I'd appreciate an idea of what's going on."

"We'll talk over dinner," she announced, with a glance in Lilly's direction.

As if listening for her cue, Hester marched into the room with a pair of heavy socks in her hand. She offered them to Lilly. "Here, Miss. Not shoes or even slippers, but..."

With that breathtaking smile Mac begrudged being bestowed on anyone but himself, Lilly reached for the woolen articles of clothing. "Thank you, Hester."

"Dinner is served."

"You'll join us, Mac?" Maisie tossed out the invitation as though she cared less one way or the other. He knew better. Something was going on and he planned to stay until he found out what it was. But he also needed to talk with Lilly. He stood.

"Might I have a few private minutes to speak with Lilly?" At Maisie's arched brow, he hastily added. "I want to tell her about her relatives. The message I relayed..."

"Of course. Join us when you are finished." Maisie lowered her hand to Arthur's and the child tucked his fingers into her palm and hopped up, skipping alongside her more sedate walk. The bond between the two was tangible and Mac was struck with a sudden urge to see Lilly walking with a child, hand trustingly in hers. A child he'd planted in her belly.

So vivid was the vision he found himself snapping his head sideways to dispel it. Maisie and Arthur followed Hester from the room and he turned to view Lilly gazing at him, wide brow furrowed with confusion.

She made to rise but he forestalled her, sinking back into the chair and pulling it closer to where she sat.

"I'll help you with these socks," he proposed, no longer able to refrain from touching her, yet unable to meet her eyes.

A beat of silence, then, "Mac? What's wrong?"

Her soft voice immediately soothed him and he gathered his thoughts, tugging the socks from her fingers. "Put your foot on my knee," he urged.

When she instantly complied, all was right in his world. He eased the ridiculously unfashionable items over the length of her narrow foot, unable to resist tantalizing the high arch. Even her toes were classy and elegant.

"The other foot," he said, gently lowering the first to the floor, somehow managing not to run his hands up the length of her leg, past her knee to what he knew were firm, silky thighs.

He dealt with Lilly's left foot as he did with her right, although he allowed himself the indulgence of circling her dainty ankle with his fingers, enjoying her faint intake of breath.

"Mac." Her tone was laced with asperity and he knew he had to tell her.

"Your aunt and uncle weren't home. I don't believe Annie was either. So I spoke with your housekeeper, Mrs. Kessler."

"Oh. *Oh.*" His Lilly bereft of words? Perhaps his perception of bitter Mrs. Kessler wasn't as farfetched as he'd thought.

"She wasn't pleasant," he confided. "I had the impression she'd have shot me, had there been a firearm available."

"She's a…" Clearly Lilly couldn't come up with an epithet, and Mac was humbled by the grace and goodness of this woman. How could he presume to be a part of her life? Yet how could he not? The idea he'd had earlier had taken root and was growing with rapidity in his head.

"Well, she isn't someone I'd want anywhere near me, or you," he agreed. "And I doubt she'll pass your message on, which means—"

"That my aunt and uncle won't have any idea where I am." Lilly finished his sentence. "I can't stay. I have to go home now."

Mac was torn. He didn't want Lilly going to her relative's home with that horrible woman alone in residence with her, yet he also knew she wouldn't worry her family. He also wanted to determine what Maisie was up to and if it fit with his plans—or not.

"We could have dinner, then go," he suggested. "I had the impression your aunt and uncle were away for dinner themselves, and Annie, from what I've seen…" A warning look from Lilly made him choose his words carefully. "I'm suggesting she might still be away herself."

Resting her chin on her folded fingers, Lilly visibly considered her options. She looked so beautifully pensive, Mac wrestled with the urge to kiss her cares away. He drifted his fingertips down her arm and she jerked out of her thoughts. As her eyes met his he lost the battle raging within him since he'd come in out of the wet. In one motion he surged to his feet, bringing Lilly with him by dint of catching her beneath her elbows. Her wonderfully soft breasts met his chest with enough impact to make her gasp again as she stood on her toes.

Lowering his head he took her mouth and nearly groaned at her sweet taste. His arms wrapped tightly around her and he allowed one hand to rise to the nape of her neck, working his fingers into the wealth of her hair to steady her for his kiss as he deepened it. She kissed him back after the first surprised instant, lips parting to allow him full access to the recesses of her mouth. Her tongue dallied with his before submitting to his full exploration. When he drew back to allow them a breath, her head fell back to reveal the long, lovely length of her neck and he forgot where he was, where *they* were. Falling on her with the intensity of a starving man, he kissed and tasted every inch of the creamy flesh, pausing at the wild pulse at the base of her throat to suckle her very essence.

Held flush against him, Lilly seemed to burrow even closer and he unashamedly ground his erection into her heat, lifting her higher onto her toes to allow their natural hollows and crevices to fit together. She whimpered and breaths soughed heavily from her mouth, ruffling his hair. Mac lifted his head and gazed at her blushing face, long, dark lashes splayed across her cheeks, hair falling loose and wild over her shoulders. He had the urgent need to see her eyes.

"Lilly. Look at me."

Her lids flickered at his tone and opened, pupils dilated with need. He fell again, deep into this woman. His Lilly. His. No matter their differences and his lack. He'd make it up to her. Make it so. "God, Lilly. I…"

A discreet cough made them pull apart with as much effect as a bucket of cold water. Lilly's hand came up to shield her face for an instant before Mac reached out and took it into his own. He'd be damned if she'd be allowed to feel an instant of embarrassment. Without looking in Hester's direction, he tugged Lilly close and whispered into her ear.

"I don't regret an instant. Nor do I care who saw us, my love."

The sudden welling of moisture in her beautiful eyes nearly killed him and he panicked. Did *she* regret this? Immobilized, he vaguely heard Hester saying something about dinner.

Then Lilly blinked, raising his hand to her mouth. She pressed a kiss on his knuckles.

"I don't regret it either," she murmured.

He waited for an endearment, but when nothing transpired, he decided to be satisfied with what he'd received. "Come for dinner, Lilly. I can't wait to hear what Maisie got up to."

Lilly blinked again at the anticipation in his voice, then chuckled, if a musical drift of laughter could be called a chuckle, and smiled sweetly. "I'm starved. And looking forward to what Maisie will share with you. And then I *must* go home."

\*\*\*\*

Mac wiped his mouth with his napkin and struggled with wanting to laugh or express his disapproval. Laughter won out.

Maisie glared at him and Lilly didn't look pleased.

"Maisie, you have to know your ... confederates can only distract the leaders for the short term. I mean, the ladies have lives too, other than charming those boys. Although I applaud your ingenuity."

"I assure you, Mac. I know those *boys* as you refer to them, and if Lilly can advise whenever they have the urge to practice their mischief, then my friends are quite able to offer them an alternative."

He tossed his napkin beside his plate, the excellent meal no longer appealing. "Lilly isn't getting involved. They wouldn't spare her if they found out. I won't allow it."

"I'll thank you not to tell me what you'll allow and what you won't." Lilly's icy tone might have frozen another man, but Mac wasn't that man. "We are doubly safe for tonight. The speak has closed for 'repairs', for an indeterminate amount of time and my employees are off on a well deserved holiday. The orchestra members are also away to visit safer climes, the police are on alert, and the Knights are otherwise occupied," he said, with far less emotion. "I'm not going to argue with you, Lilly. I'll close for eternity rather than risk you."

Silence, broken only by Arthur's hum of enjoyment as he forked yet another mouthful of succulent roast beef into his mouth, filled the room. Maisie's eyes were wide with shock, but it was Lilly's response he was far more interested in. She was staring at him as though having never seen him before. Wide-eyed, yes, but intelligence was so very evident behind the look. As if she'd totally accepted his proclamation in the living room.

"You can't give up the speakeasy," Maisie finally said, her voice a near squeak. "It's your livelihood, and you must be doing well financially. I mean—"

"I can and I will," he replied, ensuring nothing but finality was in his voice. The decision

came so came easily.

And Lilly again heard him, grasped what he was conveying without the need for

further explanation. She stared at him with complete understanding, and he knew she appreciated the fact that he and whoever stood with him in any confrontation would, in all likelihood die or

be grievously injured.

The Klan was knitted into all walks of life, and its members wouldn't easily fold

under the pressure, as was evidenced by all the great men and women who died at their hands.

He had Lilly to think about now, and their future.

"But—" Maisie hadn't yet gotten the message that she had no input in the situation. Then her head swiveled in Lilly's direction and she quit protesting. "Well, I for one will miss it, Mac. I'll have to find other venues. Such a bother."

Lilly looked at Maisie. "Or you could turn your talents in other directions."

The two exchanged a long glance, then smiled. Mac felt the same discomfort as he had earlier. Thinking of these two in league … he had no intention of letting Lilly and Maisie … ah, as if he had a choice. He turned his attention to the bigger picture.

"I should escort Lilly home, Maisie. It's getting late."

Lilly became flustered. "Oh dear. I have no idea what has happened to the old, predictable, responsible Lilly. Look at the time!"

"I suspect Mac happened to you, honey," Maisie suggested drily. "Leave me your address if you will. I'd like to get together and chat."

Lilly hastily scrawled her address on the proffered piece of notepaper and passed it to the other woman. Mac closed his eyes and tried not to think about the havoc in his future. But if Lilly was in it, he'd somehow manage.

Calling out to Hester in thanks for the meal, he touched Arthur's curls and smiled as the child lifted his cheek for Lilly's impulsive kiss. Maisie touched his own cheek with her mouth and whispered, "Don't lose her, Mac."

He swept Lilly up into his arms at the doorway, ignoring her half-hearted protest. She had to realize her improvised footwear would be awash with the sogginess underfoot in an instant. Relishing her slight weight and the heat of her body, he took his time walking to the car, balancing with her as she pulled at the door handle. They made quite the team.

Easing her onto the seat he pressed a kiss on the top of her head, drinking in her scent in full, before carefully shutting the heavy door. As he sloshed around the hood of the vehicle to clamber into the driver's seat he wished he could take her to his home, to his bed.

"I really hope my aunt and uncle are there." She sounded frightened. His protective instincts surged.

"If they aren't you'll come home with me. Or I'll stay until they do."

"Thank you."

Mac gripped the steering wheel to avoid laying his hands on her. After his display in Maisie's living room he hardly wanted to molest Lilly in the front seat of his car. She deserved better. Like his bed. "Lilly, my love, I respect your need to be strong and independent, a modern woman, but I won't ever see you threatened or at risk. What you are unable to cope with, well, I'll take care of it."

She was quiet for a time, then replied, turning to stare into his eyes. "I can't tell you how much I appreciate that, Mac. I want to be your love. But I won't be bossed."

"Sweetheart, I expect we'll argue and disagree."

With an arch look, she gave him a flirtatious smile. "And I expect we'll make up."

He fairly strangled the steering wheel in reaction to her saucy face and comment before cranking the car over and making himself drive sedately to Lilly's current residence.

## Chapter Nine

Mac was silent on their drive through the rainy streets of town, and Lilly couldn't help but wonder if he was having second thoughts. He'd claimed to want her, and she'd assumed his understandable hesitation about being with her had been quieted somehow, but his lack of conversation and the strained way he gripped the steering wheel gave her doubts. Before she could create some sort of question which might shed light on his thoughts, they were in the alley behind their respective homes and he had pulled the car close to her aunt and uncle's back door.

She looked up at the house and found most of the lights to be on, each window bright in the wet gloom.

"What could be going on?" she wondered out loud as Mac turned off the ignition and bounded out to reach her door.

"When I left, it seemed the only one home was the housekeeper and she was guarding the place like a chained dog." Mac reached out to lift her into his arms again and she wondered at the many times he'd carried her today. Surely his arms were growing tired.

Without hesitation he brought them up the back porch steps and was tapping at the door with the toe of his shoe. They waited a moment but she was impatient to enter and find a pair of soft shoes so she could return to standing on her own feet. Then she'd feel more capable of having it out with Mac Adair. It was easy to meld with him when he was stroking her feet and kissing her like he'd missed her for days, but there were practicalities to be discussed. Such as his exact relationship with Maisie.

Lilly reached out and grasped the handle to find it opened easily and they entered the deserted kitchen. A

Bible lay open on the table next to a mug of what seemed to be tea.

"Set me down, please." Lilly pushed at Mac's hard shoulder and he tightened his grip in response.

"I like knowing exactly where you are."

"You know I'll be in this house at least until I can find a pair of shoes. Isn't that a precise enough location?"

"Not particularly." Even as he denied it, he was lowering her to her feet and removing his hands from her body. She immediately felt cold but resisted the urge to press back into him. Something was amiss in this house and she needed to discover the cause.

Assuming he'd follow, Lilly made her way to the hall door and pushed it open, finding her sore feet were functioning much better than she'd anticipated. As she made her way down the wood paneled hallway she was intensely aware of the man pacing behind her. She wondered what it was Mrs. Kessler had said to him. He'd already shared enough for her to know how ignorant the woman had acted. The brass sconces illuminated their way along the soft wool runner and she heard raised voices from the front parlor.

Lights blazed from the wide doorway and when Lilly entered, she stopped short in shock at the tableau in front of her. Mrs. Kessler reclined on the mohair davenport, her dressing gown and sleeping cap askew as she moaned and thrashed her head back and forth in a theatrical manner. Aunt Eula and Uncle Wendell stood at either end of the sofa, staring down at the housekeeper with matching expressions of dismay while Annie slumped in a neighboring needlepoint chair and stared at the ceiling. Uncle noticed her first.

"Lilly! You are returned to us! Look, Mrs. Beechly, she's alive."

"Of course I'm alive. All I have are a few blisters." Lilly stepped into the room and held onto Aunt Eula as the older woman clutched at her. She glanced over her shoulder to see Mac standing in the doorway, as quiet as he'd been all along. His assessing gaze went from person to person until he settled on Mrs. Kessler and he frowned.

"Who's this?" Uncle peered over her shoulder and gave Mac a tentative smile while extending his hand. Annie stood up, swayed, and sank back to her seat while giving Mac a bleary smile. She'd obviously taken the sherry from the sideboard to her room, her usual behavior when she couldn't go out.

"Uncle Wendell, may introduce you to Mac Adair. Mr. Adair, this is my Uncle Wendell Beechly and his wife Eula. Mac's the man who helped me—"

"No! That's the ruffian who assaulted me, laid filthy hands on me!" Mrs. Kessler suddenly sat bolt upright and fixed her wide eyes on Mac, all mannerisms of a near-faint conveniently erased. Aunt Eula made a squeak and pulled at Lilly while staring at the strange man in her parlor. Uncle looked around with confusion and Annie simply giggled.

A sudden bolt of fury filled Lilly with cascading heat at the woman's spurious accusation. "Stop your infernal lying, Mrs. Kessler. Mac no more laid hands on you than an angel flew down from heaven and joined you for tea."

"Blasphemy!" Mrs. Kessler raised a shaking finger and pointed it at her, or Mac. It was hard to tell since Mac was now at her side, gently drawing her away from her clutching aunt. The warm strength of his hands calmed her ire slightly.

Lilly ignored the dramatic squeals issuing from the older woman and turned her attention to her uncle.

"Mac came here earlier to inform you of my whereabouts and it is my understanding Mrs. Kessler was less than cooperative—"

"He did not! He raised his voice to me, threatened me if I said anything."

"Let me guess, Uncle. When you got home tonight, Mrs. Kessler was quick to inform you that I was missing."

Uncle Wendell nodded.

Mac kept his silence even though she knew he longed to defend himself. She wanted to kiss him.

"Mrs. Kessler concocted this drama in an effort to discredit me. After all, here I am, all in one piece just as Mac's message would have told you, had it been delivered." Lilly watched the housekeeper's face contract into petulant lines and knew her theory was correct.

Uncle gaped open-mouthed while Aunt Eula cried out. Instead of feeling triumph at finally exposing Mrs. Kessler's evil ways to her aunt and uncle, Lilly instead felt impatient to be on her way—anywhere but here. It was likely due to the warmth of Mac's body as he stood so close beside her.

"She lies. She's lied since she wormed her way into this home. It used to be so peaceful and civilized," Mrs. Kessler moaned, as she grabbed for one of Aunt Eula's hands.

The other woman tried to disentangle herself, but didn't succeed until Uncle reached out and knocked the housekeeper's grip asunder as he pried at her rough red hands.

"Mrs. Kessler, to think you would willingly put us through this torment. We could have called the police and implicated ourselves in a predicament of terrible gossip. Find your shoes and don a robe or coat. I'll call for a cabbie to take you to a hotel for the evening. You may return in the morning for the remainder of your belongings." Her uncle's decisive tone made up for all the distress Lilly had felt at Mrs. Kessler's terrible behavior.

As Mrs. Kessler wailed, Lilly turned and caught her cousin's eye. Annie wriggled her eyebrows and tilted her chin at Mac. Lilly shook her head and tried to look above it all, but it was a failure. She knew she had to look as excited and pleased as she was feeling. Without a thought for how it looked, she grabbed Mac's hand and pulled him along behind her as she left the room and ascended the stairs. She made her way to her room to find it already well-lit. Her poor aunt and uncle had been in here and likely searched under the bed and inside the large wardrobe for her.

She shut the chestnut door shut behind them and faced Mac, a smile finally allowed to cross her lips now that they were in private.

"You amaze me." Mac growled as he advanced toward her and slid his fingers along her cheeks to bury them in her hair. She tilted back willingly into his grasp and stifled a gasp when he pressed his mouth to hers. As he stroked her tongue with his own, one of his hands left her hair and trailed down her back to curve around her backside and drag her hips to his. His arousal was clear, and the answering heat she felt between her legs prompted the mad idea that they should fall upon her bed and find an intimate connection with each other, with no thought to her aunt and uncle a floor below. But first, a point of order needed addressing.

"Mac, wait."

By way of answer he shifted his hot mouth to her neck. No matter, she could still talk even though her nerves were shattering. "Are you still engaging in relations with Maisie?"

His lips slid to a halt at the base of her throat and he lifted his head to stare at her with half-lidded but alert eyes. "No."

"And you won't as long you're with me?"

He swallowed and shook his head once. "Never. It's only you."

"And I reciprocate." Lilly held his gaze with her own as she pledged her fidelity and accepted his. Mac's fingers clenched tight in her soft flesh as he stared into her soul, the dark pupils surrounded by a narrow ring of blue. She gasped fruitlessly for a deep breath.

"I want you, Lilly."

She nodded wordlessly and stumbled back, pulling him along until the backs of her trembling knees hit the bed. She was desperate for his touch, desperate to have him when she'd suffered for so many hours telling herself she'd never burn with such passion again.

"Lilly, not here." Mac stopped staring long enough to glance around her room. She wondered what he thought of her flower-papered walls, the bed covered with white lace, an opaline glass vase filled with sweet-scented roses on her bedside table. Too pretty a place for the carnal activities she desired deep in her soul.

"Then where?"

"Home with me." He kissed her again as he breathed out his request, his caress lighter and more tempting.

"Of course." She didn't care a fig about keeping up appearances any more. "Let me put on some shoes."
****

Mac managed not to toss Lilly over his shoulder and hammer his way down the elaborate staircase, past her family and self-righteous housekeeper, out the door and across the expanse of lawn to gain the privacy of his own home. He thought about it though, the fantasy heating his blood further, as Lilly slipped her feet into a pair of frivolous pumps, the gemstone set in the heel winking at him in the dim light. Lilly herself glowed, alabaster skin and flowing mahogany hair speaking to all his senses.

"There." She surveyed her footwear with satisfaction. "I might be quite plainly dressed, but I'd say these more than make up for it."

Mac thought she'd look lovelier in nothing but her skin, and those shoes, but kept that thought to himself, hoping it might play out later. "Time to go, Lilly." His voice, even to his own ears, was dark and needy, and her responding smile, eyes locking with his, made his pulse thrum.

Offering her hand, she accepted his helpful tug and together they made their way to the door. She passed through first, and he allowed himself a touch of her hip, the warmth of her flesh apparent right through the *plain* dress.

He followed her down the steps and nodded to her family as Lilly made her farewells. The uncle's mouth opened and then closed on whatever he thought to say, and while the other women stared at them, Annie with a glint in her eye, and the aunt with a certain fascination, neither said anything other than a goodbye.

And then they were out the door and surveying the lawn, the extremely wet lawn, separating the two houses. His need swept over him like a rushing wave, and he scooped her slight weight up, hitching her tightly against his chest, reveling in her surprised gasp.

"Mac! I have shoes on. You've carried me more today that I've walked!"

"And those shoes will be ruined in the wet," he muttered. His wingtips fought for purchase on the slippery blades as the grass gave before his determined

143

strides. Lilly wreathed her arms around his neck and relaxed into him, her head fitting perfectly beneath his chin. Her trust nearly made his knees crumble, but he somehow gained the porch, one shoe unfortunately sinking into the loamy soil at the corner of a flower bed.

Lowering Lilly at the threshold—he had a plan to carry her over a different threshold, in a not so distant future—he waited until she gained her balance, then fumbled his keys loose to work the door open. The tumblers clicked as loud as gunshots in the sudden silence. Had she changed her mind? He raised her chin with one finger and gazed into her eyes.

"Lilly? Do you want this?"

One delicate brow lifted and what could only be described as a sultry vixen come hither look suffused her features. "I suggest you cease all this carrying about and playing the gentleman card, sir."

The savage unleashed, he took her lips with his, walking her backwards into the hall, the door slamming behind them with such force the leaded glass made a thunking sound. Their hands moved frantically over one another, peeling away layers of damp clothing to allow their flesh to press more intimately together. Lilly moaned deep in her throat, and Mac pulled away to allow them both a breath. He spun her to the long divan placed along the wall, the plush burgundy fabric beneath the glow of the sconces displaying Lilly's pale form beautifully. He dropped to his knees beside her, and suckled one pebbling nipple into his mouth, palming the free breast with hand.

"Please…" Lilly's torso arched and he slipped his other hand beneath her to hold her firmly against his ministrations, the silk of her gliding over the splay of his fingers, the air pungent with the scent of her arousal.

He wanted to make this good for her, and momentarily thought of coaxing her upstairs to his wide bed, but his need was too great and Lilly forestalled him, her fingers working through his hair to hold him to her.

Pulling his mouth free, he nuzzled his way over her stomach to nip at the jut of her hipbones, holding back a smile as she shivered and shuddered. She tensed as he pressed open her thighs, the evidence of her excitement slicking her folds. He set his mouth upon her and she shrieked against the stimulation.

"My god, Mac!"

He required no further encouragement, pushing his hands beneath her buttocks to raise her to a feast of his senses, tart yet sweet juices coating his lips and tongue as he lanced into her opening, then traced the pouting nub at her apex. Lilly's moans and whimpers were but background noise and he forgot how his knees protested the unforgiving hardwood and the ignominy of making love to Lilly in his foyer, working that tiny bundle of nerves until she screamed his name and her release.

As she subsided and the clenching of her sex gentled, he pressed a tender kiss upon her mound, easing his way up her body until his cock slipped against her wet heat. Lilly opened her eyes, long lashes drifting upward as she gifted him with the sated gaze of a well-satisfied woman. Even as she tilted her mouth to his, a small hand crept between their bodies to grasp his weeping member and press it against her core. It pushed inside, almost of its own accord, and the slight give at her entrance was like a sweet kiss, but Mac could wait no longer.

Snapping his hips, he drove into her depths, the hot, clenching length of her channel welcoming him home. Groaning, he tore his lips from hers to press his forehead against her shoulder, feeling her arms wrap around him to pull him closer, her thighs slipping up to encompass him. He ground his teeth against coming, not wanting their coupling to end, thrusting over and over into Lilly, into his beloved.

Tendrils of heat built in the base of his spine, travelling to his pelvis and the tightly drawn up skin of his testicles, a warning he could no longer ignore. Grinding against her, he managed a few more final thrusts, then poured his seed deep. Lilly arched once more and hugged him so tightly he thought he might crush her beneath him, her channel awash and trembling with liquid heat as she joined him in climax.

His entire body felt boneless, all his muscles lax, and his brain was incapable of forming coherent commands against the lassitude engulfing it. Somehow he managed to shift both he and Lilly slightly to their sides on the suddenly too narrow piece of furniture. They were still joined, and he was reluctant to change that fact so he remained still, holding her close and listening to her breathe. Her wealth of hair, gleaming like treacle in the yellowish light, wreathed over his upper arms and shoulder, a soft, silken whisper.

At last, she stirred, her breaths no longer as labored and fast paced.

"I love you, Lilly. Never forget that."
****

Was it possible she'd heard him correctly? Lilly tried to un-muddle her brain but it was slow going considering how overcome she was. Her heart was hammering, everything between her legs was hot, swollen, and wet, and the hard length of Mac's body pressed to hers on this narrow couch was enough to make her want to swoon. Again.

"What?"

"You heard me."

Lilly couldn't resist smiling at his aggrieved tone. Trust a man to profess his love after crisis and then refuse to repeat himself. The dark expression on his face prompted a very unromantic giggle and Lilly found herself stifling her sounds of amusement. Her whole body twitched in his arms as she tried not to laugh. Mac tightened his grip and leaned over her, a scowl on his tan features. Unable to look away from his inquiring eyes, Lilly gasped for breath and something to say to placate him. His movement and her stifled laughter dislodged his member from its haven in her body and his fluid leaked onto her thighs.

"You didn't use one of your covers. You do love me." Giddy with his declaration and unable to suppress the tiny stab of hope that a baby might result, Lilly strained for a kiss until he relented and leaned over to give her one.

"Woman, you try my patience."

"And you please me to no end, beyond reason." Lilly decided to say nothing more. Mac looked uncomfortable with his precarious position on the davenport. Time to move on to a new location better suited for talk of love. Her Daniel had told her he loved her when they'd been standing in the apple orchard as petals fluttered down around them and somehow that sweetness had suited their young and innocent lives.

Lying naked with Mac after carnal intimacy was quite a different setting for such tenderness, but somehow this felt more authentic to the person she truly was inside. She was glad he'd recognized it in her. Only with Mac Adair would she have ever found herself in this situation. "You'd please me very well if we could find a more commodious piece of furniture to continue this conversation."

Without a word, Mac responded to her request, perhaps happy to have a task. He rolled to his feet and drew her along with him in an effortless movement and she marveled again at the perfection of his physique. Rather like a bronze statue, all firm and dark red-gold. Some parts half-firm. She couldn't resist a look at his member as he released his grip on her to lean down and gather up the clothing they'd strewn about in their frenetic joining just minutes before.

He gave her an inscrutable look as he handed over her shoes while the rest of her clothes remained folded over his arm. Sensing the dare behind his gesture, she stepped into her heels slowly, both to ease past her blister and to prolong the movements of her body as he watched.

For once, Mac played the gentleman, he didn't tug her into his arms, but instead gestured at the stairs in the hall, the dark wood gleaming in the light from the newel post lamp. No carpet on the steps, so Lilly walked carefully, very aware of Mac following close behind and gazing at her bare legs, her buttocks, and the cleft between. Just the thought of making love with him again, very soon, made her knees wobble and heat build between her thighs.

"Stop." Mac's voice throbbed into her ear and Lilly halted, her heels clicking on the bare wood of the wide stair. A prickle of awareness along the flesh of her back and then the press of his warm, bare skin along her body, his thighs to her, hips pressed tight, firm muscles of his chest to the curve of her back as his arms circled around her in an embrace. He was a step below her and his rigid member pressed between her thighs.

"Feel what you do to me?"

"Yes, Mac." Her voice trembled out on a shaky breath as she widened her stance to allow him to slide in closer to her wet heat. "You feel what you do to *me*?"

His mouth crushed into the skin covering her shoulder and her whole body rocked with the sensation. Teeth and tongue worked at her sensitive flesh until she gasped out loud.

"I'd take you here, from behind just like this, if these stairs weren't so damned hard and bare."

His growled desire made her knees weaken and she nearly collapsed in front of him. His arms tightened and his hands splayed across her belly and breast to mold her to his body, his member swelling against her wet folds. She trembled and tried to catch her breath, marveling at how quickly everything faded to only him and the promise of his body.

"I don't fancy bruised knees on the morrow. The lack of soft furnishings in this house is irksome."

"I did purchase some towels at Gregg's before I encountered you and that sap." His matter of fact tone made her chuckle and she thrilled with the memory of how he'd come to her rescue. With one last caress, he released her and she stumbled forward up the stairs, no longer capable of the self-control to walk slowly.

She remembered where his bedroom was. In truth, a vision of it had lingered in her mind since she'd left it so distraught before. His bed was there, coverlet pulled tight against the mattress and she remembered how she'd opened to him, reveling in his strength. Turning away from the sight, she saw Mac enter and place their clothing on a solitary wooden chair pressed against the wall. A battered trunk alongside it completed the inventory of furnishings.

When she crooked her leg up to reach for her shoe, he stopped her again.

"Leave them on."

His sparkling blue eyes intent on hers, Mac approached and she yearned for him but something demanding welled up within her. If he touched her, she'd be pliant and impaled in moments and that wasn't exactly what she had in mind for them.

"Now, *you* stop."

He halted, one winged eyebrow raised at her imperious tone. Taking a breath as deep as she could, Lilly walked to the trunk, deliberately flexing her legs in her glittering shoes as she did so. Reaching down to the chair she pulled up the first available garment, Mac's silk shirt, and laid it on the top of the trunk. She sat down on it, the slippery material cool against her sex as she tilted her knees to the side and crossed her ankles as a lady should. What she was planning was unladylike in the extreme, but she shivered with anticipation nevertheless.

With a beckoning motion she called him over and he walked to her, halting a half a step too far. Looking up at him, she grasped his hips and pulled him close, his now rigid shaft close enough for the attentions she intended. As she slid one hand to grasp its base, Mac shook his head, his thick dark hair swinging along his temples, one lock obscuring an eye.

"No, Lilly, don't. You're too good—"

She only hoped she was good enough. His protests ended as soon as she touched her lips to the wide, rounded tip, the scent and taste of him musky and compelling. His body shuddered under her hands and she drew him deeper, stretching her mouth to accommodate him. Hard and smooth, his texture was fascinating. She couldn't stop herself from running her tongue along him both to taste and feel.

This wasn't her first time, but Danny had never been partial, so she glanced up at Mac to gauge his reaction. He stared down at her, a slight line between his brows. Not knowing if he was enjoying or enduring, she released him from her mouth, his silky tip grazing her lips as she spoke.

"Do you like this?"

One rough nod from him and she returned to her caresses, growing more bold with her lips and tongue when Mac's hands plunged into her hair and he pushed his hips her way. How far could she… Lilly relaxed and closed her eyes, drawing him in as deep as she dared and humming with satisfaction when Mac groaned and shook. His member pulsed from her lips to the back of her tongue and she swallowed convulsively, not sure how close he might be to pleasure. Salty droplets of his essence coated her tongue and she swallowed again, his taste as powerful an aphrodisiac as anything dreamed up in Sultan's harem.

"Lilly, please, release me." His guttural cry, so far from his usual controlled tones, was too much for her and she shook with pleasure, the bud hidden between her tightly clenched thighs aching.

\*\*\*\*

Mac knew he should pull out of Lilly's sweet mouth before he disgraced himself but she felt so amazing. His hands lifted of their own accord and his fingers found their way into her tresses, palms cupping her head. She looked a temptress, confident and strong as the heat of her lips and tongue drove him higher. Ladies didn't do this sort of thing and if he was a gentleman he wouldn't let her continue but…

Lilly took him to the back of her throat and swallowed again and Mac forgot about ladies and gentlemen and social niceties. His lady had thrown aside social convention to pleasure him. He roared his release, his body shuddering and black dots obscuring his vision. His shaft slipped from Lilly's reddened, swollen lips, and her tongue lapped him clean like a kitten's. Her face was the picture of satisfaction. He once again dropped to his knees, burying his face against her sleek thighs. He wrapped his arms around her to hold her close. Her hands drifted over his back in soothing movements and he heard her whisper her love.

When he thought his legs would hold him, he straightened, at once loathe to lose her warmth, and got to his feet. She tipped her head back and studied him, feminine satisfaction on her features. Drawing her up with her hand in his, Mac led her to his bed, pulling back the coverlet to urge her beneath it, then strode around to join her on the other side.

They drew together, their flesh still dewy from all the exertions of their efforts and he tucked Lilly's head on his shoulder, entangling his legs with hers. The room was dimly lit and he decided to leave the lamp, although being with her in darkness had a certain draw. He eased a hand between her heated thighs, thrilled when she willingly parted them to allow unfettered access to the soaked flesh. Lubricating his finger in the wetness he found the pearl of her sex, working it with whisper-fine movements until her breath caught and she rose up to his touch.

Increasing the pace he rubbed harder, watching her carefully, attuned to her body. She slipped into release with a shudder and a quiet sigh, her lashes fluttering in concert with the pulsing of her folds. He stroked gently until she settled, then kissed her nose. She stared up at him, and he fervently hoped to never give her cause to lose that look.

"Mac?"

"Hmm?"

She hitched closer and he could feel her breath against his throat, a feeling he wanted to fall asleep to and awaken to for the rest of his days.

"My uncle is going to confront you. Inquire as to your intentions." Beneath the humor, he detected a faint note of worry. He pressed against her.

"I would think they're clear, sweetheart. We've some things to sort out, come to some arrangements given our opposite view of life, but I have every faith we'll see it through."

Lilly relaxed and his heart swelled at the sign of her trust. Oh, they'd squabble like cats. Lilly was too bright and opinionated to merely acquiesce, but that was part of her charm. And he'd learn to accept her thoughts and opinions because she humbled him with her integrity and need to do right. Listening to her deeper breathing, feeling her body slacken as she slipped into slumber, Mac let go of any misgivings and followed her.

## Chapter Ten

Lilly felt quite the slattern. She was barefoot, her hair hanging down her back in a loose knot, and her only garment was one of Mac's soft linen shirts. Knowing he'd worn it the day before and the faint scent of his skin imbued in the fabric both conspired to make her feel like he was embracing her even though he was across the room.

As she made herself familiar with his kitchen, he watched her from his post at the table, a cup of coffee in front of him and the morning news unread at his fingertips. She liked knowing he was silently observing and she had faith he approved of what he saw as she cracked eggs in the only large bowl he possessed. While she'd been extremely impressed with his newly-installed refrigerator, its meager contents had narrowed her choices for breakfast down to eggs or toast. She'd decided on both, and was watching his toasting appliance with a wary eye. She'd never used an electrical one and was cautious about the whole process. Aunt Eula had an older model that required a lot of attention, but Mac had the latest version, which he claimed would turn the bread on its own.

Thinking of her aunt led her thoughts to her family and Mrs. Kessler's awful scene the night before. She searched for something to whip the eggs and had to resort to a salad fork. As she beat the eggs, she edged closer to Mac. Sipping his coffee, he casually snaked a hand up her leg, under the borrowed shirt to allow it to rest on her bare hip. She couldn't help but quiver and it took much effort of will for her not to drop the bowl on the floor and sprawl on the table in front of him.

"Mac—"

"Don't worry about it."

"How do you know what worries me?" Arrogant man. Lilly stabbed at a wobbling egg yolk but didn't pull away from his touch.

"You're worried about your family and about the Klan. I'll take care of both." Mac gave her a satisfied look and turned his attention to the front of the paper even as his hand slid around to cup her derrière.

"Am I to be included in your plans or do you intend to relegate me to the kitchen?"

"You look fine in this kitchen. A very nice fit." He didn't look up at her but she thought she could see a quirk of a smile on those delicious lips. "Although I fear for the fate of those eggs you are murdering."

Lilly extricated herself from his grip with a harrumph of impatience. Shooting him a hot look he didn't even notice, she poured the eggs into a warm cast iron skillet sizzling with butter. As she stirred, he spoke up.

"Are you sincerely attached to this place?"

The eggs were setting up nicely so she risked a glance at him. "You mean this kitchen?"

"No. Lima. I believe I've worn out what little welcome I had."

Something close to fear clenched in her belly. Was he preparing to leave her? Leave with promises he'd send for her when he was established somewhere else? Rather than cry out in consternation, she pulled two mismatched plates from a cabinet and smacked servings of eggs on each and scorched her fingertips as she pulled the hot toast free from the wires burning it.

She dropped his plate in front of him, directly on top of the newspaper touting a new cigar factory opening and he gave her a bland look. He eyed the other plate of scrambled eggs she was still holding with caution.

"Is that for me, too?"

"It might be if you aren't careful."

He chuckled at her warning and reached out one of his big hands to wrest it from her grip as he captured her waist with the other. Before she could work up a strategy to struggle, he had her astride his lap, her sex vulnerably exposed.

"I asked if you are attached to this place, Lilly. Give me the favor of an answer."

Lilly stiffened and gasped as he cupped his hand between her legs and she knew he could feel the sudden wave of heat and moisture his touch provoked. Unable to maintain her distance, she rocked her hips as her fingers dug into his shoulder muscles.

"I care for my family and organizations."

"And me?"

The need he allowed her to see in his dark eyes weakened her more than any intimate caress might. The upwelling of powerful emotion made tears prickle in her eyes and the breath catch in her chest. "You know I love you. I told you last night. After."

"But that was after, you weren't quite yourself." Mac emphasized his words with a stroke of his fingertips along her slick folds. She couldn't help her shudder in response, but his skill at lovemaking wasn't going to weaken her reason.

"You made your declaration under the same circumstances and I don't doubt *you*."

"True." Mac's searching look softened as he leaned forward to kiss her, his hand still busy between her legs as she squirmed and moaned against his mouth. Perhaps she *would* be on the table in a moment. She only hoped he'd shift their breakfast plates aside before he plunged into her.

A sudden rapping at the back door startled them apart and she turned to the un-curtained window with a squeak. Mac immediately rose and lifted her away from the noise, his body blocking any view she had of their unexpected visitor.

"Stay back. My men are nearby, but something might have happened to them."

Fear filled her with ice and Lilly stood where he placed her, hidden behind the edge of an oak cabinet. He reached on top of the refrigerator and retrieved a gun. She drew in a horrified breath, shocked by the presence of a firearm so casually stored on top of an appliance.

Mindful that Mac perceived a threat, she shrunk against the wall as she watched him approach the door. He slid to the doorframe at an angle so he could peer out and perhaps avoid being seen by that dark shadow behind the pebbled glass of the back door's window. Crouching, he reached out and flung the door open, bringing his weapon to the startled face of Uncle Wendell.

The older man's eyes crossed as he stared at the barrel of the revolver and he took a few tottering steps backwards and tipped off the top step of the back porch with a high-pitched cry.

Lilly let out a shriek and rushed to the door and down the steps to him, heedless of her bare feet and legs. She pulled at the tails of the shirt to cover herself as she crouched down to help Uncle Wendell up off the slate walkway. Mac emerged from the house, the gun hidden once again. He was wiping his hands on a towel and with a warm flush she recalled what he'd been holding before he'd grabbed the weapon.

With Mac's easy assistance, Uncle Wendell was soon on his feet and inside the kitchen, assuring both of them he was quite all right, merely startled. Lilly knew she was blushing. It was obvious she and Mac had enjoyed carnal relations with each other judging from her early morning presence here and her lack of appropriate feminine attire. She thought her dress was upstairs on the chair, but in their morning exertions, which had utilized said chair in an entirely satisfactory way, it might have ended up under the bed for all she knew.

"Mr. Beechly." Mac was as sober as a deacon as he held out a seat for his visitor. Lilly gladly sank to a chair opposite, grateful the tabletop would conceal her lack of lower body garments. Her Uncle was pale and blinked frequently as he glanced around the sparsely finished kitchen.

"Could I get you some coffee?" Lilly offered, but didn't rise when Mac rested his hand on her shoulder. Uncle Wendell nodded once, his gaze on Mac's possessive gesture. She stayed in her seat as Mac went to the stove and poured another mug and gave it to the other man with the ease of a man who'd poured and served multitudes.

Her uncle took a polite sip as Mac settled back into his seat and slid his breakfast plate to the side.

"Lilly, it is good to see you. At what time may I expect you'll return home this morning?"

"After breakfast." Lilly felt certain on that point. Beyond the next few hours of her future she was less assured. Mac slid her an amused glance and she frowned slightly at him, unwilling to become embroiled in a debate in front of her uncle.

Uncle Wendell cleared his throat, smoothed down his vest that had ridden up over his paunch when he'd fallen, and turned his best businessman's glare on Mac. Lilly knew her uncle's business adversaries would shift in their seats and gather their ledgers close under the older man's scrutiny, but Mac blithely took another sip of his coffee. Lilly did her own nervous shifting. The bolt of lust she felt was difficult to repress in front of company.

"The reason I'm here is to ascertain your intentions toward my niece, Mr. Adair. I made a vow upon the loss of her husband that I'd see to her safety and reputation. Mrs. Beechly and I had thought Walter might... But that wasn't to be. Last night's meeting was so highly irregular I failed to observe the proprieties."

Yes, a middle of the night confrontation with a small-minded bigot and Mac's quick footwork leading her from the house would undermine Uncle Wendell's control of the situation—anyone's control. Lilly turned to Mac and waited for his response as she cradled her own cup of coffee in her hands, the gentle ache between her legs growing as she looked over Mac's long and skillful fingers.

"My intentions toward Lilly are quite honorable, Mr. Beechly. I hold her in the highest regard and will strive my utmost to please and protect her."

Uncle Wendell made tut-tutting noises as Lilly reached under the table to touch Mac's knee. His hand immediately swept down to cover hers and she held him as tight as she could. Yet again tears threatened to fall and she wanted to throw herself into his arms and demonstrate how much she loved him.

"As admirable as the vigilance you just displayed was, I'm not certain why you'd need a firearm to protect her, Mr. Adair. You could take pot shots at the gossips, but that would only make the surviving old biddies' tongues wag harder and land you in jail. I suspect the gun was more a result of your line of enterprise than anything to do with Lilly." For all her uncle's appearance of affability and slight absentmindedness, he was an astute judge of the world at large. A man didn't start and successfully run his own oil-refining operation and think like a nit-wit.

Mac leaned back in his chair and crossed his arms after she released his hand with reluctance. Lilly realized he looked very disreputable in his collarless linen shirt and battered canvas trousers. Had Uncle Wendell noticed he didn't have any shoes on? Mac was altogether delicious to her no matter his attire or lack, but at the moment he was not in quite the same sartorial league as her uncle's properly tailored light wool suit and spat-covered shoes. Although there was a certain amount of grass and fine dirt on his trousers, the result of his fall.

"My line of enterprise, as you call it, will soon be transformed into something much less volatile. I'll never allow Lilly to suffer for any of my past actions or associations."

Tired of being left out of the conversation like she wasn't even there, she decided to speak up.

"Uncle Wendell, I respect and appreciate your concern. Mac has my trust and loyalty. You've always complimented me on my sound judgment and I hope you'll extend him your friendship and support." At that Mac leaned her way and caught her eye as he placed one warm hand on her thigh. Catching his fingers with her own, she lifted her and Mac's twined hands to the table top in a mute show of her decision to throw in her lot with him. She'd be with him in his kitchen, on the sidewalks as they walked down the streets of Lima, and in the seat next to him on whatever conveyance they chose to take them into their future.

Uncle Wendell studied their joined hands and smiled, a welcome benediction.

## Epilogue

Mac leaned back on his elbows, the buzz of insects and the muted sounds of birds a perfect back drop for a lazy, summer's afternoon rest. Lilly lay curled at his side, the blanket beneath them both an extra layer of softness over the grass. She was fast asleep, long lashes resting against the curve of her cheeks, sweet lips slightly parted. His growing baby was taking its toll on Lilly's previously unlimited energy and he felt a surge of primitive, male satisfaction to think he'd made a child in her. Not that he'd dare to take complete credit, for she'd remind him of her extremely willing role in the deed. Deeds.

They were resting close to the edge of the woods, near the old trees that had stood for over a hundred years. Trees his ancestors might have hunted beneath. Lilly had promised they'd find the blackberries she'd craved, but their bucket was empty.

The past months had been the best of his life—selling the speak, his mansion, and investing the proceeds in the railways and oil fields. The Knights turned their attention to other hapless victims and he would never regret moving his Lilly out of the line of fire. She'd warned him that day, and Maisie had bought him time, but those misguided fools wouldn't have been dissuaded for long.

Besides, the sale had facilitated their quick marriage and move to Lilly's farm. He hadn't even minded the evidence of Daniel Townsend all around, glad Lilly had enriched another man's life while being selfish enough to have her all for his own now.

Mac wasn't much of a farmer, but he was skilled in management, understood the bottom line, and capitalized on his ability to bring out the best in people. Turning the farm into a going concern had both piqued his interest and provided the challenge he needed, without breaking the law, a fact that had Lilly's approval. And he absolutely wanted Lilly's approval.

His old doorman, Dennis, assumed the role of foreman quite proficiently, surprising no one but himself, and almost all of Mac's former employees were employed in one manner or another. He continued to offer work to the less fortunate and the farm was dotted with small residences housing individuals and their families who had never had pride of place in their lives.

Lilly had her truck garden and was managing to turn a profit with the help of her partners, all local women pleased to have the opportunity to make some ready cash with their eggs, preserves, and fresh produce. In Lima, she had taken over the top floor of a pharmacy where she sponsored classes for less fortunate women on all manner of topics, from preventing conception to the proper sterilization of bottles if babies did arrive. Her aunt pretended it didn't exist and her uncle covered the rent while Maisie used her network of associates to ensure sessions were well-attended.

He winced a little to think of the mischief Lilly and Maisie sometimes got up to, but, like him, they were champions of the underdog and he had to watch how he remonstrated with her lest she remind him of his own endeavors.

"Mac?" Lilly's eyes fluttered open and her lithe body stretched. He brought her closer to his side, relishing her scent and the warmth of her.

"Yes, sweetheart?"

"Are you day dreaming?"

Heart swelling, he pressed a kiss on the top of her head and laid a hand possessively on the curve of her belly.

"I've no need for day dreams, Lilly. I'm wide awake and living one."

She tilted her head back to stare into his eyes, her love unmistakable, and gave him a smile that suggested they might want to retire to the farmhouse and seek privacy.

"How strange a coincidence to share the exact same dream." She rolled awkwardly to a seated position and rubbed her lower back, her braided hair falling over her shoulder.

Rising to his feet, easing Lilly up with him, Mac ducked down to gather up the blanket before settling his free arm around his wife's shoulders. They walked, side by each, together, toward their home.

By dint of his birth, all of this should have been prohibited. The rise from the depths of poverty to become a successful and wealthy businessman, winning the heart of the most incredible woman in the entire world, fulfilling that woman's dreams as well as his own, and in the end, attaining a depth of satisfaction he'd never believed possible.

John MacDonald Adair welcomed the future.

The End

PROHIBITED

www.lynnraewrites.com

www.perielizabethscott.com

Evernight Publishing

www.evernightpublishing.com